She is the moon, wrapped in my darkness, yet she is my light...

-    R.H Sin

TWISTED King

TWISTED CITY DUET

BOOK II

RIA WILDE

Prologue

Marcus

I stare down at the body, pale skin stained red with blood, blackened by dust and ash. The doctors rush around the bedside, inserting needles into her skin, pipes into the throat, bandages to stem the bleeding before they can get in to operate and fix this mess.

I feel no remorse as I stare at my daughters' lifeless body, at the translucent skin, slowly leaking life. I need her to survive, not because of the familial tie we share, I couldn't care for that, this *thing* is no daughter of mine. A traitor, a liar, a cheat. She may hold my name but that is all that links us.

But she has use yet.

My daughter, as vile as she is, is a beauty, nonetheless.

Her appearance has been whispered between the ranks of my men, and then further still, I've heard the tales of the Valentine with copper hair and green eyes and I know how very valuable she is. What she can bring me.

Alexander Silver thought he would get to keep what rightfully belonged to me and here I am, proving him wrong.

He's likely ash and bones now, burned up and incinerated by the flames that I know are still devouring the building, the heat tearing through the club as easily as a knife slicing through butter. It's a shame he won't get to witness all the things I have planned for his precious little Wren.

It would have been satisfying to see the pain break the man when he watched me take his city *and* destroy his girlfriend right before she's shipped off to God knows where with God knows who.

I don't care what happens to her, but I hope she suffers.

All I care for is the resource she will bring.

I am not naïve enough to believe I can take this city alone.

Before, I chose the wrong person to help in my scheme to claim Brookeshill from the Silver's, now I've learned from my mistakes.

Any men left still loyal to Silver will perish, the rest can join my ranks and watch this city rise from the ashes under my rule.

The Syndicate will die.

The Silver name will die.

And once the blood on the streets has been cleansed, it will be my name they whisper, it'll be me they bow down to and my face that haunts their dreams.

So, whilst the doctors and the nurses battle to save the life that will help claim my rightful place, I turn from the room and pull out my cell, dialing the number only listed as Heart in my phone.

"Valentine," his English accent rasps through the earpiece.

"It's time."

1

Lex

My eyes sting with the smoke that swirls around my face, my lungs screaming for fresh air. Each breath burns as I inhale, my throat raw, a metallic coppery taste coating my tongue.

I can feel how weak I am, my limbs heavy with fatigue, body broken and bruised. Blood drips from my chin, my fingers, sliding over my ash covered skin like crimson snakes, mingling in with the dirt, rubble and dust beneath my palms. Fire crackles wildly to my left, the flames devouring everything they touch and it's only a matter of time until they reach me. I can feel the heat searing my flesh, making my blood boil and clothes cling to my skin, drenched in both my blood and sweat.

Bodies litter the ground, bloodied, burned, broken, eyes staring lifelessly at the ceiling where the disco lights continue to pulse green, red and blue across the club. Somewhere close by sirens wail and horns blast, people talk and scream.

I push up though my legs are too weak to hold me, and I smash back down, grunting as the pain floods through my limbs, but I try again and again, one thought pushing me. One thought that erases all else.

Get to Wren.

Wren.

Wren.

"Over here!" I recognize the voice though it's muffled, like it's being spoken from behind a pillow. My vision blurs with my fight to get up, my head swimming but then hands grasp my arms and I'm hauled to my feet.

"Lex!" Ryker's voice shatters the fog inside my head, like the blast of a horn, it cuts through the mist until I can finally think clearly. His face swims before mine, forehead crinkled with a frown, a deep crease between his brows as he studies me, picking out every injury.

"Wren." Her name is a rasp from my throat, voice wrecked by the smoke and pain, a plea directed at no one and everyone all the same. My little bird. *My sweet little bird.*

"I know, boss," Ryker continues, dragging me towards the door. His feet kick at the bodies on the floor, people who were once dressed in their finest now bloodied and dead, some no longer whole and only vaguely resemble a human body, mangled and torn up, limbs missing, burns that have eaten away at their skin and muscle, exposing organs and bones beneath.

Death. So much death.

My chest constricts, my lungs squeezing and I hack, my body trying to rid itself of the toxins filling my lungs. I taste the coppery tang of blood on my tongue, mixed with smoke and ash. The stench of the dead and burning flesh assaults my nose but it isn't that that makes my stomach churn, it's the lingering scent of her on my skin, her blood now mixed with mine coating my hands. That's what makes my stomach roll. She's gone.

I will kill him for this.

I will Kill Marcus Valentine even if it's the last thing I do.

This is more than the city. This is more than my life. I will level this entire place to the ground.

They always talk about the monster who runs this city, they tell ghost stories to scare children into staying in their beds and stop teenagers from wandering the streets at night, and if it's the monster they want, then it's the monster they'll get.

I will tear them all limb from limb, I'll let their blood coat my skin, wearing it like a cloak and I won't stop until I have my little bird back in my arms.

When we finally make it through the exit I suck in my first breath of clean air, coughing onto the sidewalk with each inhale. The street is lit up and bathed in red and blue light, fire trucks and cop cars skewed in the road as paramedics tend to those who were lucky enough to escape the carnage whilst firefighters tackle the raging inferno that has already burned through half of the building and is now spreading to the buildings on either side. Even out here, I smell the potent stench of burning skin, and hair. My eyes sweep over the chaos, noting the panic, the fear that pales the emergency responders faces, the sheer terror in their eyes as they realize they can't save everyone and the people still trapped within those burning walls are going to be consumed by the raging flames.

It was carnage. Destruction.

A paramedic rushes to where we stand, takes one look at me and widens his eyes before he grabs a hold of my arm and begins to steer me towards an ambulance waiting in the middle of the road whilst he shouts orders that I don't listen to.

"Get the fuck off me," I growl, voice raspy.

"You're bleeding a hell of a lot man," the guy says, "You need to be checked out."

"I'll give you two seconds," I warn, "Before I blow your fucking brains out."

I had no idea if I even still had a gun on me, the blast knocked the shit out of me but even if I didn't, I'd find one and I'd make good on my promise. The paramedic lets go of me quickly, too quickly and in the weakened state that I am, I stumble, almost losing my footing until I catch myself on the side of a cop car.

"You need to get checked out, boss," Ryker comes up beside me, looking in a much better state than me. He's bloody and dirty, but he walks like he didn't just get blown the fuck up. Motherfucker is built like a steel giant.

"I need to get to Wren," I tell him, vision blurring as I limp at his side towards the underground garage where I know my guys parked the SUV.

Ryker doesn't argue, instead he helps me like the fucking broken boy I am and shoves me into the passenger seat when we finally get to the car.

I pull my cell from my pocket, "Fuck!" I growl, slamming a bloodied hand against the dashboard as the thing practically falls apart in my grip, the screen shattered, shards of glass falling away and landing in my lap.

There's no fucking time. Who the fuck knows where Marcus has taken Wren and if I don't get on it right the fuck now it could be weeks before he decides to resurface. I don't have weeks. Wren doesn't have weeks.

This ends now.

And if he so much as hurts a single hair on her head I'll be sure to make his death long and painful. They'll be no mercy, I will flay him alive and make him eat his own flesh.

My head pounds, a steady thump, thump, thump that mimics my own heart pumping in my chest. I should have been checked out, I'm no fucking use right now but Wren... She needs me. A King will always protect his Queen, and I may have failed this time, but this motherfucking God is vengeful.

The drive back to the compound is rough, my consciousness slipping in and out the entire time and by the time we pull into the driveway, Ryker parking as close to the door as he can get, my lids are hooded and heavy and my body has all but given up. Numbness has started to creep in, through my fingers and my toes, blood dripping like a crimson river over my skin, staining the seat beneath me.

"Shit, Lex," Ryker hisses, pulling me from the passenger seat. I can't make anything out, the house ahead of me blurs in and out of focus, the gravel beneath my shoes crunches but it sounds as if I'm under water, drowning in the dark waters of the ports that surround this city, unable to break the surface. My legs barely carry me, limbs too heavy and sluggish. My feet scuff on the floor, tripping over the gravel as we slowly make it up the stairs and into the compound.

I can't die. Not yet.

Wren.

Get to fucking Wren.

Ryker drags me through the foyer, my blood dripping onto the floor, before he drops me unceremoniously onto the couch.

What the fuck happened!?

It was safe. *Safe.*

I flinch as the memory of Wren's shooting slams into my brain, the blood, so much blood, stemming from that whole in her abdomen, leaking out over her dress, seeping through her fingers. And then her crumbled and broken body, laying in the rubble of her own fathers making, staring at me, eyes wet with tears.

This shit, these fucking damn feelings are going to kill me quicker than the injuries currently sucking life from my body. Wren fucking Valentine was my undoing.

But she was also the damn thing that was going to get me off this fucking couch because she needs me.

I was *her* monster.

Her demon.

Her devil.

Regardless of whether I liked it or not, there was no way I'd be able to just let her go. No way I wouldn't tear this city apart just to find her.

Ryker begins to tug at my clothes, grabbing the lapels of my torn jacket to shuck it from my shoulders.

"Easy," I growl when his frantic movements jar the injuries littering my abdomen.

"Doc is coming," is all he replies, "I need to stop this bleeding, just until he gets here."

"I'm getting her back," I say to him once I'm stripped from the waist up, the air of the house cool against my skin. The blood seeping from my wounds chills as soon as the air hits it, droplets of crimson that feel like ice rolling over my skin. This wasn't only my blood though, this was her blood, on my hands, my face, my body. It was hers.

I've never cared much for human life, I've only experienced one death that gutted me and that was my mothers, but the idea of Wren never seeing the light of day again, never giving me shit or fighting me, it cripples me. It guts me from the inside out. The organ inside my chest no longer beats for me or this city, it beats for her. It thrums for her touch, her body and without it, the thing is useless.

She told me she loved me.

I didn't deserve that, not from her.

I didn't deserve that full stop.

Loving me would damn her to hell.

I would never let her go, she belonged to me, and now I know she has given me her heart, I'll do anything to get her back, damned or not.

This city has been my all forever, until she crashed into my life, kicking and screaming. This city was my only until she stole that away from me and replaced it with herself.

This was my own doing.

All the events that have led up to the now, that was my fault.

But even the Gods made mistakes. And that is what I am.

A fucking God.

I am king.

And it's time this king goes into fucking battle. It's time this king places his queen on the throne beside him.

I'm coming little bird and together we will bring our enemies to their knees.

2

Lex

"That fucking snake," I hiss.

"You called it," Ryker huffs, sucking on a cigarette. He's not a smoker but in the last few days he's had one hanging from his mouth near on every second.

Griffin was to blame for the detonation of the explosives.

That motherfucker was going to pay. I am not easily deceived but he had me. Did he ever truly care for Wren? I would have said so but watching him now, concealing himself in an alcove in the club, in a nice little safe spot as he pressed the button and caused the whole building to explode. The explosion happened in sections, first the door, making the exit impassable, then the bar, the patrons receiving drinks being blown to pieces in the process and then in the middle of the dancefloor. Fire erupted and chaos ensued as he slipped through the carnage, unscathed and escaped out a back exit whilst the rest of us burned.

This just proves how far I've fallen.

With the footage of the club, not publicly available to the authorities, I've picked out several faces employed by Valentine though the shooting, I've realized, did not come from them. That was a whole different story and whilst his face is concealed beneath a hood and mask I already know the man belonged to the Syndicate. A hired gun to do their dirty work.

"Find him," I slam the lid of the laptop down hard enough that I hear the screen crack, "I want him in that fucking barn by morning."

"Yes, boss."

Ryker gets to work, leaving me in the compound to stew on my decisions. There's zero chance of me being in the field for at least another couple of days, I know my limits and unfortunately, I am only mortal. Several deep lacerations, broken ribs, some minor internal bleeding, burns and a concussion later and I'm still standing.

The club is gone.

Burned to the ground, along with the hundred and fifty seven bodies that succumbed in the attack. Only seven of my men died, the rest were innocents.

No one was truly innocent in this life, but they were

innocent in this war.

I want Valentine to believe I perished along with them. A lot of the bodies in the club were so badly damaged, identities have yet to be announced, giving me the perfect opportunity to remain in the shadows for the time being. With me supposedly gone, there will be no need for Valentine to hide.

He's in hiding right now, but he'll come out soon if he thinks I'm dead, after all, if I'm not around, the city is open for him to claim. If I have to pretend to be dead for a few days then so be it, I'll wait, and I'll watch until he crawls out of whatever hole he is in. My men are on the streets, in every club, bar, building and shop, waiting for the moment he rears his ugly head.

There is a clock ticking above his head and there is only so much time left until it hits zero and when that happens, it'll be my face that sends him to Hell.

I pull the footage up on my phone, watching Valentine lift Wren from the rubble. She's so broken, my little bird, her wings crushed. She's lifeless over his shoulder, I can't even see a movement in her chest as Valentine carries her away, disappearing out the door before the emergency services show up.

I managed to track them to about three blocks away but after that, the trail went dark.

Not for long.

Valentine has underestimated me.

Severely.

"In the barn," Ryker drags me from my thoughts a few hours later. "We have Griffin."

That didn't take long.

I feel a cruel smile tug at my lips as I stand from the desk, ignoring the pain that shoots through my body with the movement. There is nothing inside of me but blinding rage, an anger so dangerous there won't be a single person left to utter the Valentine name.

"Grab the driver," I say to Ryker as I head out the room, towards the back door that'll lead me to the barn. Three men flank me whilst Ryker grabs the item I have asked for.

The night air is humid when I step out into it, the heat pressing down onto me, stifling, heavy. A sweat breaks out across the nape of my neck as I cross the lawn towards the barn. Impenetrable darkness surrounds us here, the only light this far from the house comes from the moon and the stars above.

I push the door open, the old wood creaking with the movement, hinges protesting. I'll have to sort that, I think casually as my feet scuff across the dusty floor, grit and dirt sending small clouds of dust to bloom in front of me.

Four men are strung up before me.

There's no kindness here, no chairs to be restrained to, instead they're tied up to the beams in the ceiling, arms together above their heads, tied at the wrists as they dangle there, only the tips of their toes brushing the ground beneath them.

Griffin is in the middle, his face a bloodied mess, swollen, blue with bruising and blood stains his clothes.

One eye meets mine, the other swollen shut and he curls his lip, baring his teeth to me. The other three hang there like the limp dicks they are.

With a blade in my hand, I press the tip of it into my forefinger, swirling the razor edge against the skin until a bead of blood wells to the surface and streaks down my finger. I ensure I hold my weight even though my muscles scream and protest, I don't show a weakness. Not in front of the enemy.

"I didn't think we would be seeing each other so soon, Griffin," I say calmly, sitting myself in the chair that's been placed directly in front of the bodies. I survey them. They look like animals, strung up for the slaughter, each one broken in some way.

"Fuck you, Silver."

I tut, sucking my tongue against my teeth, "You had even me fooled," I continue, "That's not an easy task so I will applaud you there."

"She wasn't supposed to be there," he hisses, "she was supposed to be on the balcony!"

I shake my head, "You Valentines' are always making mistakes."

17

"And what about you, huh, Silver? You're the reason Valentine has her!"

I stand abruptly, my fury boiling, "No, Griffin, you are. She was safe with me until you went and fucking blew up my club!"

"You really believe I would have left her with you?" Griffin sneers, "You're a fucking monster and she is innocent. She doesn't belong in this war."

"I really thought you'd be on her side, but you've been Valentine's little bitch this entire time."

"I have no loyalty to Valentine. I did what was necessary to get her away from you."

"And that didn't work out so well did it."

Griffin doesn't answer. I wonder how much he knows. Did he know the Syndicate had her shot only moments before he detonated those explosives? Does he know I held her bleeding body in my arms when he pressed the fucking button? Does he know where she is?

I retake my seat, kicking up my leg until my ankle rests on my knee, pushing down all those thoughts, calming the raging sea of emotions rising like a wave inside me. I pull at the cuffs of my white shirt, straightening the sleeves and then I twist the leather cuffs around my wrists, making sure the silver emblems are facing upwards. On one is a feather, a recent edition to honor my little bird, on the other, a wolf. Fierce. Loyal. Deadly and cunning. I hadn't worn them in a long time, an old Silver tradition I didn't see fit in the now however, I had recently changed my stance. We had never been defeated before and every Silver before me wore their cuffs like crowns. I would be no different.

Griffin watches me through his one good eye.

"Tell me Griffin," I drop my arms, linking my hands over my stomach as I lean back in the chair. I'm moving too much, disturbing my stitches, causing my joints to twitch and roll and jump, lighting fires under my skin as the pain bursts through my body. "Did you get a good look at what you had done? You claim to care for Wren and yet you blew up the building she was in."

"Fuck you, Silver, I care more for her than you ever will. You dragged her into this war, what happens to her now is entirely your fault."

"You're correct," I nod once, "I brought her into this, but I wasn't the one who handed her to her father. Valentine has plans for her, what are those?"

"You assume she is still alive."

Those words turn my blood to ice, it freezes inside my veins and causes my heart to slow down enough to make me truly believe I may pass out. She's not dead. She can't be. A roaring begins in my ears, so furious it drowns all else out as images of her body, pale, broken and dead flashes inside my head.

Not my little bird. Not my Wren.

I don't show any of that though. I don't show the emotion on my face or in my body as I lean forward, dropping my leg to the floor as I rest my elbows on my knees and rest my head in my hand, feigning boredom.

"Is she not alive, Griffin?"

The words are acid on my tongue, leaving a vile taste in my mouth. She wasn't dead. Valentine was using her for something, and he needed her alive. After everything that has been done to get her away from me and into his clutches, there is no way he's killed her. Unless she didn't survive the gunshot and the explosion. Panic claws its way into my chest. It is entirely possible that she did not survive.

His nostrils flare.

I grit my teeth as the next words spew from my mouth, "Tell me, come on, tell me how Valentine broke her so bad and dumped her body somewhere. Paint the picture for me. Tell me she is now just a corpse, rotting in a ditch somewhere."

He doesn't say a word.

He can't lie. Not about this and his silence is louder than any words he can speak. Wren isn't dead.

I truly believe he cares for Wren, in a twisted, fucked up kind of way. He wanted to get her away from me, but he hadn't banked on the Syndicate getting their shot in first. He hadn't banked on her being so damaged afterwards she was easy picking for her father.

He wanted to destroy me, my men, so he could get to her himself, but shit doesn't always work out the way we plan.

"Your silence is awfully loud," I stand, "and now I need some information from you." I flick the tip of the knife towards him, using it to point, "we can make this easy, you just need to talk."

"She will hate you for this," he growls.

"She might, but ultimately, she'll forgive me. Do you want to know why, Griffin?"

He doesn't answer but his teeth grind together, his fingers twitching above his head.

"Because I have her heart, Griffin. She chooses me. *Me.*"

3

Lex

Ryker hands me the driver as I snatch up one of the timber screws from the stack to the left. Griffin watches, that one good eye narrowed in my direction. He tries to hide his fear but I smell it, I live on this shit. His fear is palpable, it coils in the air like a phantom snake, wrapping around us, making my heart thump with adrenaline, the blood course through my veins like a freight train.

The guy to his left is awake, he's as quiet as a mouse though, too afraid now he's in the vipers nest.

"So, Griffin, where is she?" I ask as Ryker casually lets the guy down, unhooking the ropes binding him to the ceiling so his body drops to the floor with a hard thud. Ryker's face is an impassive mask, mouth set in a straight, unemotional line but I see the darkness and vengeance in his eyes. He wants them to hurt, he wants to make them pay.

The guy groans, too fucked up to even fight or move on the dirty ground. The sound of a body being dragged across the floor fills my ears but I don't dare look. I keep my gaze trained on Griffin though he watches my man move the body to a steel table where he's then strapped down, his shoes and socks stripped from his feet.

"What are you doing?" Griffin asks, ignoring my question, eyes flicking from me to his guy.

"I think you're forgetting your place here," I back myself towards where his guy is prepped and ready for me. "Answer my question, *where is she?*"

"I'm not telling you shit, away from you is better than anything else."

"Even with Valentine?"

"He's the lesser evil."

"In this life, Griffin, choosing the lesser evil is not always the smart choice."

I line the timber screw up with the guys heel, pressing the tip hard enough into the skin that a bead of blood wells to the surface. "I'll give you one more chance," I say, "One more Griffin, I don't give many chances so think yourself lucky."

"Fuck you, Silver!"

But his eyes are wide with terror, his voice shaking with the fear that rattles through his body like an earthquake. This is just the start of my revenge. Only the beginning of what I am going to do to those who have crossed me and Wren.

"I'll go through each of your men, Griffin, until I get to you, until I get the answers I want." I promise as I line the head of the driver to the screw and press down on the trigger. The sound is deafening to begin with but then the scream that erupts from the guy on the table overpowers that. His agony bounces off the walls, loud, painful, twisted. The screw slices through his skin, blood splattering as it spins through muscle and cartilage, vibrating against bone. The guy passes out long before I get it all the way in.

"You're fucking sick!" Griffin bellows, his fear a stench that stains the air. I breathe it in sharply.

The skin on my face is slick with blood, war paint that I smear over my face as I turn back to Griffin and a wicked smile pulls my mouth up. I no doubt look manic, a complete psychopath and if they didn't fear me before, they will now. "Tell me where she is Griffin."

"Fuck you!" He bellows.

I tut with a sigh and gesture for Ryker to wake the guy up. It takes a few minutes, but he eventually comes to, tears of pain rolling down his bruised face, leaving clean tracks on his otherwise dirty face.

"Griff, man," he begs, voice broken, "Tell him, please."

I line the second screw up, his limbs twitching, trying to escape but don't they know? There's no escape from me.

"Yeah Griff, tell me." I mock.

"I don't know!" he yells frantically.

I sigh, the driver dangling in my hand, "That's the wrong answer."

The screw goes in just as the first, bloody, loud, violent. My hands are coated in this guys blood, his cries of torture ringing in my ears like music.

I bounce from foot to foot, "Doesn't it make you feel alive, Griffin?" My laugh echoes through the barn, "doesn't it make you feel powerful? You hold all the keys here, Griffin, you can make this stop."

Griffin furiously lashes against his restraints, his body swinging. His hands have long gone purple from lack of blood flow, the wounds across his body clotted now and the blood dried to resemble the color of rust.

"You're a fucking psycho"

"You're probably right," I nod my head with a sigh, turning a little to watch Ryker unbind the guy from the table and drag his bleeding ass back to the ropes where he proceeds to hang him like a prime cut of meat. Blood drips down from the wounds in his feet, the skin blackened. I mean that shit's gotta hurt, right? "But I still don't hear you talking, so really, who is the bad guy here?"

"I don't know where she is, Silver!" He cries, "I don't know!"

"Why do I think you're lying, asshole?"

"I'm not!" He pleads, "He knew I found her and didn't

tell him, the club was a test, okay!? To get back in his ranks. If I didn't, he would have killed me."

"You should have let him end you."

"I don't know where she is. He keeps moving, the last location I know about was in the city centre, an apartment block but underneath, it wasn't an apartment listed on any map."

"The address?"

He rattles off an address which Ryker writes down.

"That's good Griffin," I tell him.

"You're going to kill me, aren't you?"

"I am, Griffin."

He hangs his head, "You'll never find her, Valentine's smart."

"All you fuckers have underestimated me," I step up to him, pulling the knife from the holster attached to my belt, "Every single one of you. You've come into my city, started a war that you have no hope of winning and have expected me to what, give up? Let you all fuck me in the ass whilst you take my city and my girl?"

I nod to Ryker who makes quick work of finishing the other guys hanging from the ropes. They're no use to me, low in the pecking order, they'll have fuck all information I could actually use. Griffin's eyes widen as he watches each of them die, a single bullet to their foreheads, quick and easy. My face remains impassive. Taking life is as easy as the air I breathe.

We come into this life screaming, bloody, traumatic and it fits that we exit it the same way.

"You've called the monster now, Griffin, don't be surprised that he's answered."

I step up to him, tilting my head a little so I can look directly at his face. Fear swims in his eyes as I raise the blade and rest it against his neck. I don't waste a minute, there's no more words to say as my knife slices across his throat, cutting through skin, tissue and muscle, his windpipe opening up to me like a yawning jaw. Blood pours from the gash, sliding through the gaping wound and down his front, staining his white shirt red. His gurgles and muffled cries last only seconds as he bleeds to death, sucking in air that'll never reach his lungs and then his head droops and his body goes slack and the life finally drains from his body.

"Clean it up," I tell the men stationed sporadically around the barn, "make sure this one," I point to Griffin, "Ends up in public view. I want Valentine to see what he has done."

They get to work as I grab a cloth and wipe the blood from my fingers, the two bracelets around my wrists clipping together to make a tinkling noise that is almost melodic. Death permeates the air, the stench of blood and sweat heavy. Ryker joins my side as we exit the barn back towards the house.

"Ten minutes," I tell Ryker, "then we go to this address."

With the blood cleaned from my skin and the clothes on my back fresh, I step from the SUV, holding back the wince as my body cramps with pain. There's no time to recover, no time to sulk in the compound when my little bird is out there waiting for me.

The apartment building ahead of me looks like any other, a high rise but it's clean and tasteful, no wasters or low lives hanging outside. There is a security call button outside the large glass doors listing apartments from one to sixty five but they are not what I am looking for. There's no button for an underground apartment but that's hardly surprising and from the research I've done, this building belongs to a real estate agency here in the city, one that isn't on my payroll.

I laugh to myself, cheeky fucker.

It's non-descript, to look at you'd never know there was a secret apartment below and so instead of going through the entrance, we round the building, my guys following and find the fire escape. It's locked but that shit is easy to get through and then we're in a stairwell. To the left is a set of stairs leading up to apartments above and to the right is a supply closet.

The building is silent all around us but the sounds of our boots on the hard floor echo up the stairwell. Ryker shoots the lock on the closet door and three guys slam through into the darkness.

"Clear!" One yells and we follow in, taking another set of stairs down to yet another door though this one is

28

unlocked.

The apartment inside is huge, a ten bedroom mansion fit onto one floor. Opulence and money drip from the walls, chandeliers made from crystal hang from the ceilings and art worth more than most cars people drive hang on the walls. I sweep through the place, finding it empty of any human presence but Valentine left a lot of shit behind.

He must have been tipped off that we had been given his location and ran. He gets it. I'll go to all and any lengths to get her back.

"Search it," I tell the guys, "I want everything empty. I want him found!"

They don't dawdle, splitting up to search the rooms whilst Ryker and I head through to the office room.

A huge oak desk sits against the back walls, and as it's underground, there are no windows so he's compensated by installing lights every few inches against the wall. A huge cabinet sits against one side, bottles of aged whiskeys and brandys sitting on the shelves. On the desk is a glass still half full with an amber liquid and there's a half smoked cigar in the ashtray though there's no laptop, no phone, only a note sat in the centre of the desk. I guess he knew I wasn't dead then.

Silver.

Give up. I have Wren.

Give me the city and you can have her back.

If you don't, I can assure you nothing pleasant will be in her future.

Today is Monday, you have until Friday to surrender.

Choose wisely.

M Valentine.

4.
Wren

I've never felt pain like it.

My whole body is alight in agony, pure, unfiltered pain that runs through my bloodstream like wild fire ripping through a forest. My hands are restrained by leather binds at my sides, my ankles in much the same state at the bottom of the bed. To my left an IV drip is hooked into my arm and a machine beeps to match the pace of my frantic heartbeat. If I wasn't in this room, I might believe I was in the hospital, but hospitals don't look like this.

There are no satin curtains, or million dollar works of art hanging on the walls, there aren't crystal light fittings or fur rugs in a hospital. A window to my left shows a courtyard, I can see out onto a manicured lawn with a stone fountain spurting clear water into the air. The sky a perfect cloudless blue.

The door to the room bursts open and a woman, dressed

in blue hospital scrubs rushes to my side, silencing the machine still beeping wildly at my side. She checks the IV, picks up a clipboard attached to the end of the bed and then grabs some equipment from a box at the end on a counter.

"Where I am?" I rasp, my voice scratchy and hoarse from lack of use. Even talking hurts. Everything hurts.

Her eyes bounce to me, but she doesn't say anything as she positions the blood pressure sleeve around my arm and hooks something to my finger, pressing a button on a device she holds in her hand.

"I'm talking to you!" I growl, "Where I am!?"

"Please," She whispers, "I'm not supposed to talk to you."

"Who told you that?" I ask.

She shakes her head.

I don't remember much.

We were dancing, Lex and I, and then we took it to a more private area, the office.

I felt free, wanted, aroused and then, pain…

It tore through my abdomen, ripping through my gut and then blood. So much blood. I still remember the way the warm liquid seeped through my fingers, coiling around the digits and soaking through my clothes.

Lex was there. He was frantic.

The calm beast was finally rattled.

He looked... terrified.

I suck in a shocked gasp as I recall the way he looked at me, gone was the darkness in his eyes, the soulless stare and it was replaced with a fear so potent it took my breath away. He was scared for me.

After that I can't recall what happened. There was a loud bang, a boom really but what happened!?

"Where the fuck am I!? Where's Lex!?"

"Please," the nurse begs, eyes wide with fear.

"You can leave," a hoarse voice says from the doorway. My eyes snap to the newcomer.

"Who are you!?" I snap.

The guy steps into the room, dressed finely in an Armani suit, the color of midnight. His dark hair is streaked with silver but it's his face that gives away his age. Late fifties but looks much older with deep groves that wrinkle his skin. His eyes are the same color as mine, an emerald green flecked with gold and he's clean shaven.

I already know who he is, I see myself in that face, the eyes, the shape of his nose, but I want him to confirm it.

Lex is a monster. I've always known it, his darkness is

something that swirls around him, it's his aura, his shadow. He's a terrifying creature but this man, it goes beyond that.

There is nothing there. No soul. No heart. No emotion. It's just a shell for a beast to inhabit but this beast cannot be tamed or reasoned with.

He looks at me like he would look at dirt beneath his Italian loafer, a speck, nothing, worthless.

You'd be stupid not to fear a man like Lex but not fearing a man like this would be lethal. Where Lex may hesitate, this one would not.

It's not because he looks particularly evil, it's all in the way his dead stare bores into you. It feels as if he's sucking out my soul, feeding off my life force.

"Oh, daughter," the sentiment is cold, it's not said with any fondness at all, "I've kept you away for too long."

My nostrils flare and I fight against the restraints holding me in place despite the pain wracking my body. The nurse flees the room, I can't even blame her. My fight or flight has kicked in and I've always been a fighter but right now I want to run, as far and as fast as I can away from this man.

My father.

Marcus Valentine.

He comes closer slowly, casually, with his hands buried into the pockets of his suit trousers, his watch glimmering in the light of the room. He stops at my bedside and picks up the chart, looking over it.

He whistles through his teeth, "It looks like you took quite the beating."

"He's going to kill you," I hiss through my teeth.

His low chuckle bounces off the walls.

"He has to find me first, but don't you worry, daughter," he reaches forward and even though I snatch my face away, his hand still touches my hair, pulling the strands away from my face and coiling them around his finger, the ringlets dull and limp. "I've made sure he understands what's at risk here."

"What did you do?"

"I've made him an offer he can't refuse, of course."

I meet his soulless eyes, trying to figure out what he means, what he's saying but there is nothing there. His face may as well be made of stone.

"What offer?" I breathe.

He tsks loudly, shaking his head, "Nothing to concern you, it doesn't even really matter now."

"Then why not tell me!?"

He cocks his head, his finger trailing down the side of my face that's sore and bruised, the skin of his finger snagging on the raised and dry skin on my cheek.

"You really are a beauty, Wren," he says absentmindedly before gripping my chin and forcing my head to the side, his fingers biting into my flesh hard enough that my cheeks cut against my teeth. The taste of blood coats my tongue. "You chose the wrong side, do you know that?"

"Any side is better than yours," I manage to grit out, despite the unrelenting grip on my face.

His fingers bite in harder and before I can even think, even react, he removes his hand and strikes it across my face, the pain flaring in my cheek bone.

Motherfucker.

"You're lucky," I bury it, the agony, the shock, I give him nothing even though the deep rotted fear shakes me to the core, holding my heart captive and the pain in my body makes me want to scream, "I'd kill you if I could."

He gets in my face, his nose pressing hard against mine, so close his face blurs and I can't make out a single feature. His breath reeks of whiskey and smoke, a stench so heady it makes me gag.

"You're all going to fall. You've made a mistake, daughter of mine and it's time you remember you're a fucking Valentine."

He snatches away from me, storming from the room.

"Get her ready," I hear him say.

"She's too weak," a feminine voice replies shakily, "She

needs to recover."

"Do I look like I give a fuck!?" Marcus bellows, *"Get her ready."*

It's minutes before someone reenters the room. Minutes of deafening silence and then the nurse from before scurries in, her head hanging low, a defeated sag to her shoulders.

She begins to unhook the machines, slowly, one by one before she heads round to the other side, placing latex gloves over her fingers.

"What's going on?" I ask her, hoping she'll answer me.

Her glazed eyes bounce to mine, shining with emotion, "I'm sorry."

"What is he going to do?"

"I don't know," she answers, "If you get the chance, you need to run, okay? Run, Wren, as fast as you can."

I'm not a runner. I don't hide from my demons or my enemies but the fear rolling from her makes me question everything I've ever known. I felt it when Marcus came into the room, the man wasn't just dangerous, he was beyond that. I didn't want to admit it but given the chance I'd likely run. I knew my boundaries and fighting off Marcus Valentine wasn't something I could do on my own.

There's a sting as the nurse pulls the IV from my arm before she presses a cotton pad to the small puncture hole, stopping any minor bleeding.

"Can you tell me what happened to me?"

"Concussion," she sighs, "a gunshot wound to the abdomen, we got the bullet out and it managed to miss your organs, so that's good, you lost a lot of blood though. There's a fracture in your wrist, several lacerations, bruising, swelling."

Shit.

I felt weak. I felt hurt. But those injuries weren't something I could simply get up and walk away from. I was in no state to fight. No state to argue.

And I knew, I *knew* Valentine had much worse planned for me.

There was the promise of violence hanging in the air and that was all for me.

5

Valentine's man drags me from the room, still dressed in a hospital gown and I can feel my limbs protest with the movements. My abdomen twinges and pulls, the stitches moving too much, I can feel the wound beginning to reopen, the warmth of my blood seeping through the front of the gown.

"Stop," I beg, but he doesn't, if anything, the grip on my arm only increases, his pace becoming faster to the point my feet drag more than step across the carpet. It burns my bare feet and the pain pulsing through my body makes the edges of my vision turn black, a thick fog pushing in at the sides.

We walk for what feels like forever, down endless corridors and past opulent rooms, until we hit a door and I'm forced down a steep flight of concrete stairs. The steps are freezing beneath the soles of my feet, grit and sharp gravel biting into my skin. When we make it to the bottom, the hallway before me is barely big enough to fit two people side by side, the light dim and almost murky.

We only stop when he roughly twists me and shoves me into a small room.

The door slams behind me, the noise ricocheting off the walls. A single, metal framed cot sits in the centre of the small cube of a room, an old dirty mattress on top with a single, thin sheet folded at the bottom. No pillows.

The light buzzes overhead, dangling there from a wire that has seen better days. There's condensation on the walls, tiny beads of water that cling to the concrete walls and it smells of mold and rot, the stench of death permanently etched into the walls. There are dark patches staining the floor and the color gives away to what it was that was spilled.

Blood.

A lot of blood. Through the door I hear feminine whimpers, cries for help, screams and sobs. There are more women down here, I didn't get a good look when he dragged me down here, too focused on trying not to pass out from the pain but now I'm alone I hear them. I hear all of them.

What the fuck is this place? I swallow down the panic and fear rising like bile in my throat and scan the room once more.

Apart from that rotten bed, there isn't much else in here. There's a sink that used to be white but is now stained brown and yellow, the tap constantly dripping water. There are no windows in here but I'd already figured that. We were underground, way underground with no way out apart from that one door we came through.

I press my hand to my abdomen, looking down at the red splotches. With the door closed, I pull up the gown to check it out. There's a thick padded plaster over the stitches, but the blood has seeped through that and onto the gown. I carefully peel away the edges, hissing as the adhesive tugs at the bruised skin around the edges. The wound is clean but it's bleeding, not terribly but I can see the stitches have pulled away. The area around where the bullet tore through me is purple, black, yellow, matching the rest of my body. Bruises and scratches cover a lot of the parts of my body that I can see but I didn't doubt the parts I couldn't see looked in much the same state if how sore I was, was anything to go by.

Pressing the gauze back down gently, I trudge to the bed, gritting my teeth as I lower myself onto the cot, too weak to care about the state of the furniture. I suck in a breath, holding it as plumes of dust puff out from the mattress, stinking of rot and decay and only when it settles do I let out the breath.

"Please," I hear a voice just outside the door, "Please no!" The voice appears young, far too innocent to be in a place like this. Loud bangs and further cries echo down the halls, growing quieter as whoever it is, is dragged further away.

My stomach rolls at the hideous ideas forming in my head, prostitution rings, human trafficking being the main ones. Girls went missing all the time, never to be found again and it's things like that, the insidious darkness that prays on young girls and women that usually get them. Most get falsely declared dead, no evidence to ever suggest such a thing happened and once they're declared dead, they're forgotten, leaving them to this evil.

This world is a cruel, harsh place, the people in it even more so. There are monsters everywhere, there's no escaping them and sometimes you have to join them in order to survive.

I've chosen my monster.

And it isn't Valentine.

He may be my blood but he is not my family.

Given the chance I will pull the trigger myself.

Exhaustion tugs at my consciousness and I can feel my body sagging, bowing over to the side as I try and fail to fight the grips of sleep. The sheets smell of damp, a musky sent that makes it hard to breathe easily but it doesn't stop my eyes from falling closed.

Just five minutes. I can take five minutes to rest.

I bolt up in the bed to the sound of a scream so gutting it tears through me. Goose bumps rise on my arms and my stomach churns with the noise. Very male grunts and groans fill in the gaps between the cries and I have no doubt in my mind exactly what is going on here.

Valentine truly was evil, dabbling into this sort of thing is a sure way to have your soul ripped from your body.

Bile rises in my throat, burning my tongue but I don't vomit, there's nothing in me to even bring up, so I sit there and I listen, unable to help the poor girl down the hall.

Eventually her cries die down, becoming gurgled and muffled but the man in her room continues, his booms of pleasure turning my blood to fire. I want to kill him. The burning rage blinds me, makes me into something I've never been and I welcome it.

I welcome that darkness, the claws of it seeping into my mind as I imagine ripping the mans' throat out with my bare hands, watching him bleed on the floor. Reveling in the warm, crimson liquid coating my skin, relishing how quickly the light drains from his eyes.

What would Lex do? Tear out his organs whilst he made him watch? Cut off his cock and feed it to him?

Lex was a lot of things, but I knew he wouldn't do this. The man may be evil, but this level of evil is saved for the likes of Valentine. The ones so deprived and soulless not even hell would want them.

A door slams and before, I couldn't figure out where the sounds were coming from, but the slam is right next to me, the room over. It'll be why her cries were so loud and his grunts so nauseating. His feet pound heavily on the concrete floor and my heart leaps up into my throat when they stop right outside my door.

I swear I hear his heavy breaths through the door. My fear is thick but there is no damn well way I'll let him touch me.

 I brace, fully prepared to use any means necessary to protect myself and hold my breath, waiting. After a few *long* seconds, their footsteps retreat and they head up the steps, the door slamming as they close it behind themselves.

I climb from the cot, my legs weak, barely able to sustain my weight as I creep towards the door, pressing an ear to it. The handle doesn't move as I press it down, but I already knew that, I wasn't stupid enough to believe they'd leave it unlocked.

"Hello?" My voice is quiet, too quiet so I speak a little louder. "Hello?"

A cry answers me.

I wait for a guard or something to bang on the door, demanding silence but when that doesn't come I speak again, "What's your name?"

Her sobs break me, it's filled with an anguish that goes soul deep, fills your body with so much sorrow you could weep for years.

"Tessa," she replies.

"How long have you been here, Tessa?"

I was going to get this girl out, all of these girls out, even if it was the last thing I did.

"I don't know," she sniffles, "A long time."

"Can you remember the day you were taken?"

Three breaths of silence and then, "December eighteenth. My twenty second birthday."

Six months. She's been here *six months*.

"Okay, Tessa," I say, trying to put as much comfort into my tone as possible, "We're going to get out of here, okay? Do you hear me?"

"We're not," she replies.

"We are."

"No, we're not. We're all going to die down here."

Not a fucking chance.

I had no idea if Lex was coming and it didn't even really matter if he was, I was no damsel, I didn't need rescuing, I mean a little help would be nice, but I was getting out of here with or without him. There was no way I was dying like this, like a rat in a sewer. And none of these women deserved this fate. I was getting us all the fuck out of here.

"Hey!" A boom of a voice shatters the delicate silence between us, "Quiet down!"

Tessa whimpers. These walls are paper thin, the doors even more so. You can hear everything, the footsteps, doors creaking, floorboards groaning above. It's why I notice the second set of boots hitting the steps. Slow, calculated, casual and then his voice penetrates the wall and my blood runs cold.

Father is back for another visit.

"Is my lovely daughter causing problems already," he tuts as if I'm a petulant child, "well, I suppose it's time to teach the girl some manners."

The words are so carefree, so casual and nonchalant you'd simply think it was a father scolding a six year old and not a twenty three year old.

The last visit wasn't pleasant.

This visit is going to make that one look like a walk in the park.

6

Lex

A twisted grin tugs at my mouth as I rise from my crouching position, cocking my head as I stare down at Jameson, or what used to be Jameson. You could hardly recognize the man now.

I flick my eyes to Ryker who stares down at the man impassively, like this is an everyday occurrence to him. But I guess it is, in this life, shit like this happens all the time.

Okay, maybe not, but we're not shy to the scent of death.

Jameson has been crucified to the wall inside Valentine's old apartment. A big old *fuck you* to Valentine.

Ha.

He thinks he can threaten me.

No.

Did I believe he'd do something to Wren, damn right I did but I also wasn't stupid enough to believe he'd simply hand her back either.

That little note was a bluff.

He wants my city, but I know he won't give Wren back.

Would I give it up for the woman?

Probably.

And that shit terrifies me.

Jameson's white shirt is no longer white but stained scarlet red, the buttons undone to reveal a large 'S' that's been carved into his chest, the wound so deep you can see the layers of fat that cover the muscle underneath. I'd like to tell you he was long dead when I graffitied his skin, but he wasn't. His screams of pain still ring inside my head, his pleas for mercy left unanswered as the tip of my blade sliced through his skin. He should have known there would be no mercy in this.

We did at least, manage to get some information from him before he croaked it.

An English organization, no names but there were plenty of English that could be the culprit. It would take some time to figure out who it was that was working with the vermin, but off the top of my head I couldn't think of one that would sink so low or be so stupid. They were all big. The English and the American's had very little do with each other.

There was no need.

He wouldn't give up the location of Valentine, not for love nor money and I had to hand it to him, that was loyalty. He still had to die.

Blood runs down the walls and I dip my finger into it like it's paint, smearing the thick substance over the note Valentine so lovingly left for me.

I have left one in return.

Run.

That's it.

Because if he didn't run, if he didn't heed my warning, there would be only pain in his future. I wasn't going to let him live, even if he did run and I would chase. I'd make a game of his demise, a sport for my entertainment and fuck, would that be entertaining.

My little bird was missing from my side, from my bed, her attitude and her soft body was absent and I was slowly going crazy without her.

I don't know how it happened or when it happened, but she was under my skin, in my black soul, a light cutting through the shadows that is my life.

I *needed* her and I've never needed anyone.

This shit sends men like me batshit, like an addict gone

too long without a fix.

I didn't know where she was. I knew she was alive and that at least settled some part of me but how bad was she injured? What was Valentine doing to her?

It was these questions, the ones that haunted me when I tried to sleep, when life became quiet, the silence too loud, whilst I was waiting and watching for the next lead, the next word, the next anything where I pictured her. And I saw what he was doing. I saw her bleeding, bruised, broken. I saw her spirit and her fight leave her wild eyes and it pumped me full of rage.

It was blinding.

I allow my mind to wander back to catching Jameson, I revel in his screams, how we dragged him from his comfy bed in the south side of the city, how he kicked and he screamed whilst tied up in the trunk of the car. He threatened us to start with but those threats soon turned to pleas. I replay how Ryker held him down as I slammed paperclips under his fingernails, remembering the feel of his blood on my skin. But it was only when the tip of that knife sliced through his flesh, permanently marking him with the S that he started to talk but it still wasn't good enough.

He eventually died, sooner than I had wanted but a fitting end for him at least.

This apartment has been turned upside down twice, the remnants of the last time still strewn across the floor, glass smashed, holes in the walls, papers crumbled and littered over the varnished hardwood.

Jameson was useless.

They're all fucking useless. A sudden burst of fury has my fist slamming into the wall next to where Valentine's second hangs. He's long dead, gone cold and blue and yet I wish I could see a flinch. I need the fear. The fucking terror. It drove me. I wanted suffering and pain. *I wanted them all to fucking pay.*

My men back from the room as my anger bursts from my body, what wasn't destroyed before now is, the desk, the furniture, even the hundred year old bottles of whiskey on the shelves. All but Jameson and the note except now it's embedded into his sternum, held there by my switch blade.

Blood coats my hand like a second skin, warm, slick, crimson. I feel it on my face, my throat.

I've never lost a single thing in my entire life, but I was losing everything now. Every-fucking-thing.

I can feel emotion clawing at my windpipe, my tongue, drying it until it sticks to the roof of my mouth, my heart pounding inside my chest to the beat of a frantic drum.

Wren. Wren. Wren.

That's what my heart shouted.

I never thought something would become more important than my city. Than my family name but she has. She *is.*

"Lex," Ryker steps into the room, the only one brave

enough to face me down in this current state. I pick up a bottle and launch it across the room, a scream erupting from my throat, the bellow ricocheting off the walls to fill the space with an echo of my anguish. My rage. My pain.

He's just another body, not necessarily in the way but a body there anyway. So easy to destroy. A life that can be snuffed out beneath my thumb with just a simple flick of my wrist.

I'm this fucking close.

I imagine what it'll be like when I finally have Valentine in front of me. What it will feel like to inflict wound after wound onto him.

He's smart to hide.

I wish he wasn't, but I had to hand it to him as much as I didn't want to.

There wouldn't be anything to stop me if I saw him. I wouldn't care if we were in public, fuck they can broadcast it for the nation, I'll kill him still. I'll make the whole fucking city, the whole country watch as I enacted my vengeance.

A calmness settles over me as I tilt my head side to side, working out knots that have formed in the muscles. Rolling my shoulders, I loosen the muscles in my back and flick a glance back at my work.

I give it an hour after we leave before this little scene is put before him.

I'd love to stick around and see just who it will be to deliver my message but I have no time.

For every day my little bird is missing from my side, I'll triple, *quadruple* the amount of damage I do to his men.

Going for his right hand now was a little hasty, I should have waited but my control, it's slipping. And he can only be to blame.

Taking a deep breath through my nose, I close my eyes, inhaling the stench of death that tinges the air with a metallic tang, it was the smell of a man losing himself to his own demons.

And this time, there was no pushing them down. No restraining them. No concealing them from the people of this city.

They wanted the monster.

I'd give it to them and make them wish they never even stepped foot in this city.

This was war.

And it was a war I wasn't going to lose.

7

Wren

"Ten years," that's the greeting I get from my father as he steps foot into my little cube of a bedroom, "Ten years I've known that man. Do you understand how hard it is in this way of life to have someone like him stay loyal to you for so long?"

After he came to my room earlier, throwing around his air of menace, he didn't act on it. He promised to show me some manners and never delivered.

I stand from the cot, holding in the wince that wants to give me away as my body twinges in pain. I was weak, that much was obvious, we both knew it but showing that weakness, that vulnerability was another thing.

I had no idea what he was talking about and wasn't going to ask.

He stands in the doorway, a menacing shape blocking my escape but I can see into the hall beyond him.

What I failed to notice before was the door opposite my room, no doubt the same door that's repeated all the way down this hall. They look to be originally painted green but with age, they have deteriorated and now rust spots and peeling paint make up their exterior, an ugly shell to hide an even uglier interior.

My father, Marcus Valentine was a trafficker. Amongst other things.

I wonder idly, as we stand face to face, the air between us sizzling with suppressed rage and fury whether we could have ever had a connection.

I mean, at the end of the day, this man is a part of me. His darkness is in me one way or another, but I don't look at him like I want him as a dad.

Benjamin Lawson was my father. He raised me. Granted, he wasn't much of a father either and tried to kill me, but he was still more of a father than this man would ever be.

Did I regret it?

Not even a little.

I wanted nothing to do with this man.

This monster.

"Restrain her," Marcus says, jerking his chin towards me.

Two men enter the room, holding heavy set chains as

they advance towards me.

"What?" I say, "Afraid I might hurt you?" My voice rings with all the confidence I don't have, but my body gives me away as I start to back up, the edge of the cot hitting the backs of my knees.

He laughs, "Oh daughter of mine, you don't scare me. This is so you don't move too much. That'll take away from the fun."

My nostrils flare as a healthy dose of fear injects itself into my bloodstream. I can't show him that weakness, I can't show him how much he terrifies me.

There's no hope of fighting them off, no hope of winning any battle with them as they wrap those chains around my wrists tightly, the metal cutting into the skin and drag me towards the wall next to the bed. They link the chains to the steel hoops I failed to notice in the walls, pulling them tight so my arms are stretched out at my sides and on my knees, my face pressed to the damp wall.

I'm not able to control my breathing, I can't stop the frantic way my heart pummels inside my chest, beating against the walls of my ribcage, so hard I wonder if it's possible for it break through the bone.

I pull at the restraints, hearing the metal clang loudly, the sound mingling with the footsteps drawing closer. Measured. Leisurely.

"Ten," Marcus muses.

I finally give, "What are you talking about?"

"Alexander Silver wants you back," he answers.

Lex. *My monster.*

I say nothing as I laugh though nothing is funny.

"If Lex wants me back, *Valentine*," I spit the name as if it doesn't belong to me too, "You best give me to him."

"He's not in control anymore."

Or so he thought.

Lex was smart, too smart, calculating, categorically evil, and Marcus was underestimating him badly.

Lex would be on a war path.

To get to me.

He'd made it clear I belonged to him, I was his, no matter the cost and he may not have said the words, but I knew what I was to him.

I shouldn't want the man who kidnapped me in the first place, my heart should not beat for the man who set off a chain of events that would ultimately lead me to this very moment but clearly my heart wasn't very smart.

Not that I could blame it.

I had fallen in love with the darkness.

I wasn't going to fight it. Not anymore.

He could have me.

All of me.

Possess and claim and keep.

I was Alexander's.

"Ten," Marcus repeats.

I hear rustling behind me, but the restraints restrict my movements, I can't look back to see exactly what is happening.

I don't say a word.

"Ten," the number is repeated and then hands grab at the back of my gown, ripping it away from my body until it falls away, revealing my bare back.

The first lash of the whip is a shock and I'm not able to hold in the scream that unleashes from my throat.

The second is just as much of a shock and the third. I hear them counting.

A lash for every year.

The thin strip of leather whips against my skin, ripping it open. I feel blood and sweat rolling over the surface as the wounds open with each new laceration.

At four, the pain becomes unbearable, my

consciousness begins to slip, I clutch at it but it's loose and slimy, never quite staying in my grip.

My head sags forward on the fifth and whilst I still feel the whip hitting my skin it's almost warming, like it's gone from pain to something else entirely. I know it's there but it's happening to someone else. I see it. I hear it.

Six.

I'm sure I'm going to die.

Seven.

I see Lex's face, his fathomless, silver eyes, his amused smirk, the wicked gleam.

Eight.

I feel his hands on my body, soothing the cuts, kissing away the pain. His teeth nip at my flesh before his lips kiss away the sting.

Nine.

Fight little bird, his words penetrate through the fog inside my mind. *Come home to me little bird. Stand by my side. Be my queen.*

Ten.

You are mine.

You belong to me. Only me.

I wake stuck to the sheets, the wounds on my back clotted and scabbed over, fused to the dirty fabric under my back.

Sweat makes my hair cling to my forehead and my skin is on fire but that's nothing compared to the pain in my back, it makes the gunshot wound still healing in my abdomen a walk in the park.

I'm starving. Dehydrated.

At this point, I'm not entirely sure Marcus wanted to keep me alive.

Perhaps he just wanted me to suffer for as long as possible.

At this rate it would be forever before he put me out of my misery.

I pull myself from the sheets, squeezing my eyes closed as the sheets snag at my skin, reopening the healing wounds on my back.

I feel a trickle of blood run down my spine as I head towards the sink in the corner of the room on unsteady legs.

Turning the faucet, a spurt of dirty colored water bursts from the pipes, filling the stained basin with brown colored liquid before it finally clears.

I wasn't about to drink it, not yet at least but it would be good enough to get some of the dirt off my face and aid in cleaning the dried blood on my spine that was making my skin too tight and causing it to pinch.

As I wipe the blood from my skin, I notice how eerily quiet it is, so silent you'd hear a pin drop outside the door. The light is on in the room and there doesn't appear to be a switch to turn it off. The electricity buzzes through the wires, the bulb flickering every now and then. There was no peace in this place.

No retreat.

I knew I wasn't going to die down here, that was too easy. But there are some things that are worse than death and that was the path Marcus was leading me down.

8

Wren

For every one thing Lex did to retaliate against my father, Marcus gave it back to me ten fold. Lashes to the back, beatings, starvation and dehydration. All I was told was that Lex was destroying it all. Valentine had lost nearly half his men in recent weeks at the hands of Lex and his men, buildings and warehouses destroyed, burned to the ground, men gutted, murdered and mutilated beyond recognition. They don't hide the information from me, it's spoken aloud outside my room, them discussing how crazy Lex has gone. He's killing everything in his path.

Before I would have been disgusted, shocked and scared, but all I feel now is an adoration for the crazy bastard. He was bringing death to Valentine's doorstep and I knew he wasn't going to stop. I didn't know if he would ever find me or get me back, part of me is sure this is where my life ends but there's a glimmer of hope, a small beacon shining in the shadows surrounding me that it's only a matter of time before I'm back with Lex.

I've lost count of how long I've been here, days, weeks, months? I had no idea. The slipping in and out of consciousness doesn't help, every time I don't know how long I'm out for and there's only so much the human body can take before it starts to shut down. Not just in body but in mind too.

Give up, the small voice inside my head urges, pleads for it if only to stop the suffering. If you shut down, shut it all off then the pain inflicted won't touch you. It won't matter because you won't care. And if you don't care, death isn't so scary. If you just let the pain take you, if you just let yourself slip into that darkness, you won't ever have to emerge again. There will be no more pain, no more suffering, just a peaceful darkness where nothing can hurt you.

The threats. The graphic images, the screams and the cries, they won't matter because you don't feel anymore. You don't care.

I know if that happens everything I was before, everything I had, including my feelings for Lex will just vanish. That's if I didn't die first.

Not because they didn't matter anymore but because I wouldn't have the capacity to deal with them.

The mind is fragile.

It always has been, us humans like to think of ourselves as these super beings, strong, powerful, smart, but we have so many weaknesses. Emotion being one of them, it's what controls most of us, even those who claim not to have it are controlled by it in some way. Greed.

Courage. Fear. All emotion.

Lex tried to claim he was emotionless, he acted as if nothing mattered but everything did. His city. His control. His power. It sent him over the edge and if that isn't emotion then perhaps, I've been wrong this entire time. With everything I have learned in my twenty three years, it's that humans react on pure basic instinct. Survive. Fight. Live. By any means necessary. It's amazing what we are capable of given the circumstances. How many stories have you read about women murdering their attackers? Children no older than ten or eleven killing their parents just to survive. We want to live. To Survive. We think we could never do such a thing but the balance between good and evil has always been a precarious thing. A slight nudge to the other side will tip the scales and once you're over that edge there's no turning back. You're in a free fall, that abyss, that darkness ready and waiting to swallow you whole.

The wound in my abdomen doesn't feel as painful today, it's not as tender, doesn't seem as if I'll rip my body open if I move too much or too quickly which is a good sign. My bones aren't fairing the same fate. I ache. All of me, from the top of my skull to the tips of my toes. Muscles scream in agony from all the positions I've been contorted into, from all the flinching and tensing that's inevitable when you know pain is coming.

No amount of preparation would get me ready for what Marcus had planned for me.

It's like he took pain and notched it up a level, figuring out new ways to torture without causing too much damage. It was punishment to Lex but to me too.

Despite being raised as a Lawson and not a Valentine, I must be punished for turning on the family name. It made zero logical sense but, in this world, what was logical and rational didn't always mean what was right for them.

You're a Valentine. He'd chant through his beatings, *Wren fucking Valentine. Act like it.*

But I'd never be a Valentine. I'd rather be nothing at all.

The screams of the girls surrounding me only settles that further into my brain.

I'll let him break me and beat me and make me empty before I ever submitted to him.

It doesn't feel like much time has passed when I'm visited again. I'm still healing and sore from the last visit, the blood barely dry on my skin but the gleam in Marcus' eye this time is like none other. It's wicked and evil, devious, like the devil has entered his body and is about to inflict damage.

I brace, standing on my bare feet. The grit on the floor bites into the skin on my feet and my muscles twinge wanting rest but there is no rest here. There will be no reprieve for me.

"Your man never learns, Wren. You must not be too important to him if he keeps doing what he is doing knowing each time he does it, I punish you."

I scoff, "You don't know Lex at all."

"He's weak. Useless and unfit to run this city anymore if a bit of cunt is what has finally tipped him over the edge."

I square my shoulders, tipping up my chin.

I belonged to Alexander Silver, he doesn't share, he doesn't give up what is his. This city, it's his, and me, I belonged to him too.

It was obvious.

He wasn't a man that thought rationally, he knew what Valentine was doing and he was lashing out, unable to stop himself. If you cage a wild animal you expect to get bitten and Lex was no different. There was nothing grounding him without me by his side.

He would get to me. Eventually.

I just hoped I wasn't too far gone when he finally found me.

Lex

Blood.

So much blood.

It covered her pale skin, turning the creamy color crimson, streaking paths over her curves like snakes. She looked too pale, too thin. Her face was away from the camera so I couldn't see her face but even her hair looked limp and lifeless.

He was killing her slowly. Her heart would always beat but my little bird was being ripped away, piece by piece, shard by shard. Feather by feather.

She's strong.

A fighter.

A queen.

But there was only so much she could take.

This seemed like it may be the final straw.

The V carved into her thigh is raw and gaping, the edges of the wound bruised and swollen. He'd cut into her with a blunt knife, the edges of the wound are too rough and jagged for it to be a clean cut. There are bruises littering her skin. Purple and black showing the newer ones and yellowed and green ones showing the old. He's beating her.

Hurting her.

The need to maim has never been stronger but it's a cold kind of fury that settles over me in this second.

I'm past being angry. I'm past being uncontrollable.

It's just a being now.

The updates on Wren have been hammering in a nail for weeks. The frustration of not knowing where she is only adding to the pressure. Eventually I was going to boil over to the point of no return.

My little bird has been crushed. Her wings were breaking.

And I couldn't find her. *I couldn't find her.*

I don't think in this moment, I just unleash my rage onto the man in front of me. My fists pound into his flesh, his bones and skin breaking with each slam of my fist. I feel my own skin break from the hits, but I don't feel the pain, just the warm blood of his and mine mingling together as I kill him with my fists.

When his body sags unconsciously I still don't stop. Not until his chest stops moving and my skin is slick with his life essence.

I was close.

I knew I was.

I was coming little bird. I was.

She just needed to hold out a little longer. Stay strong a few more days.

My fist slams into the man's face beneath me, my knuckles raw and bloody but it's nothing compared to the mess in front of me. The images tear through my mind and a scream unleashes from my throat as I slam my fist down again, what was left of him breaking under my rage.

Ryker drags me away from the body when his face no longer resembles a face, just bloodied pulp and I breathe heavy, clenching and unclenching my fists. I don't feel better.

He's permanently marked *my* woman with his initials. The large V on her thigh will never go away, a constant reminder of how I fucked up.

The streets of the city were turning to chaos. To ruin.

This war was getting bigger and bigger each day, so much blood has been spilled in the last few weeks than it has in years.

Not even the rain can wash away the damage.

The Syndicate have been quiet since the attack on Wren at the club. Why would they need to get involved, after all, their two problems were ripping at each other's throats. They're probably waiting to see who wins this and then will aim for the victor.

It was clear Valentine was a loose canon.

Ainsley has disappeared. There's no way to find her, track her or contact her and I need that information she has. I won't be able to use it right now but when Valentine is dead and the war has been won, the city won't settle into peace.

Enemies don't just disappear.

They just sit and wait for the right opportunity, the right time to strike but I'd be sure to be ready for them.

And I'll have Wren by my side.

My queen.

My little bird.

"Clean it up." I order the men lingering at the edges, faces unable to hide their fear, it shines in their eyes every time they look at me, their minds wondering when I'll finally snap at one of them.

They are smart to be cautious with me.

I haven't heard from my father despite his promise to give me what he knows about the syndicate. His phone has been disengaged but I know he's still alive. He may be out of the city and away from the carnage, but my men talk. He still has ties in this city and he's pulling the strings. Making my messes go away, watching, observing.

It's why I haven't lost my shit with him yet, because despite his sealed lips, he's still helping in all the ways he can.

I can feel the tension leave the room with me, the heaviness easing as I step into the cool air of dawn. Sirens wail in the distance and dogs bark from the houses a few streets down. It's early morning, the city still sleeps, oblivious to the battle raging all around them.

One way or another, this was ending now.

The only way I wasn't getting to Wren was if I were dead.

9

Wren

Hands scrub at my skin, not in anyway gentle or soft, the bruises and cuts ache and sting with each pass of the sponge but I've become numb now. I don't feel the burning sensation of my skin ripping or the tenderness across the bruises.

My mind is gloriously blank.

The screams of the girls all around me does nothing to me anymore. Valentine's threats roll off my skin like water lapping at the shore.

His words don't bite, his threats don't elicit fear.

I'm simply nothing.

Dead but still breathing.

The same hands washing me grab at the dirty gown covering my too thin frame and rip it off, leaving me naked on the bed. I should be worried these men will do something to me, harm me in the same way, abuse the situation but they don't, instead they continue to wash my skin, removing the dried blood and dirt caked on me like paint. My eyes drop to the large V carved into my thigh.

This way you'll never forget who owns you. Not Alexander Silver. Not his men. Me.

He branded me.

Permanently marking me with his initial. My initial.

But it wasn't the brutality of the act that finally broke my mind.

No, I kicked and I screamed and I slashed at him whilst he sliced the blunt edge of the knife through my skin. I even managed to get myself some slight satisfaction as my nails left angry welts in the top of his hand.

What finally broke me was what happened after.

The memories, the only memory that occupies my mind now, begins to play. Like a fucked up film playing on repeat, the stop button broken and the movie on a loop.

I felt the blood rolling down my thigh, dripping onto the floor beneath where I was restrained to a chair. I thought it funny how every interaction with the man I was always restrained. He worried what I might do.

Smart man, I had pictured a thousand ways to kill him with my bare hands. I've imagined ripping his eyes out with my fingers and strangling him with my hands, I've pictured how his eyes would beg for mercy and how he would fight but ultimately lose.

All the lessons I was forced into had taught me several ways to kill a man with only my hands. I could even make it look like an accident if I wanted.

The pain of the knife in my flesh was like nothing I'd ever felt. The bullet in my abdomen was nothing compared to the prolonged torture of a blunt edge ripping through your skin, but I kept the pain out of my voice as I told him all the ways I wanted to hurt him.

When he was done and I was marked with the V, he looked at me like I was merely a possession, a pretty little doll on his shelf, not like I was his daughter, his flesh and blood.

"All the girls are branded," he explained, "but only my daughter gets a special kind of mark."

"Fuck you." I spat.

"So disobedient," he tutted, "So mouthy. Don't you know women are to be seen and not heard? It is the only thing you're good for."

"You're disgusting. I can't wait to watch you bleed."

He just grinned maliciously as he jerked his fingers over his shoulders, notifying the man standing behind him to do whatever it is he asked for earlier.

"Perhaps a little motivation, hm?" He cooed, "a little

persuasion. My plans are far too precious to be ruined by a bitch of a woman who can't learn to keep her trap shut so maybe this will help you learn your place."

I swallowed, knowing I wasn't going to like what I saw.

Even preparing myself for it wouldn't have ever set me up for what happened next.

The man behind him disappeared for a few minutes, but when he returned, he wasn't alone. He dragged a small woman in with him, dressed in a blue summer dress, she sagged in his grip, her straight blonde hair hanging around her face like a limp curtain, areas matted and bloody. Bruises mark her skin, cuts and grazes down her arms, her legs. Her feet are cut up, nails on her hands torn and bleeding. Marcus continued to grin as he took measured steps back.

"I believe you two have met," he told me, reaching beneath the mane of disheveled tresses to grip the girls chin. My heart pounded inside my chest and dread settled deep into my stomach as he jerked her face up for me to see.

Rory.

My best friend.

Her face had been beaten black and blue, one eye swollen, a gash across her right cheekbone, and her bottom lip split and fat. Her one good eye widened when she saw me, and a sob of pure and utter agony escaped her throat. I'd never forget that sound.

"I believe you've been listening, these walls are rather thin after all." Marcus cocked his head to the side, "my men seem to enjoy this one along with the pretty little thing next door."

The scream that echoed through the room after that could only be described as inhuman, I wailed, the pain blooming so fast and furiously it exploded out of me.

It was just me before. I didn't know these women, as much as it made me sick, I could disassociate myself from it but not Rory. Not *my* Rory. My innocent best friend who had managed to escape a life of hardships to come out on top. Not my friend who loved life, loved to laugh, loved to explore. She was as innocent as a child. And he had her.

He had ruined her.

All the screaming, the memories of the cries and pleas beat like a drum inside my head. I had listened to the demise of my best friend and I had done nothing.

"Wren," she sobbed, bloody spittle drooling from her swollen bottom lip.

Marcus reached down and gripped the hem of her dress, dragging it up almost to her underwear, and there, on her right thigh was a brand. Not cut in like mine but burned, scorched into her skin like they do to cattle.

The burn is weeks old, healed over but still raised and angry, the skin around it blackened.

"Let her go!" I screamed.

His fingers continued up, tracing the edge of her underwear, "Perhaps I should give it a go."

"Get your hands off her!"

Aurora just stood there, she didn't fight, didn't scream or cry. Her eyes are glazed over, dead, soulless. They did this to her.

"You want it to stop?" Marcus continued, pulling at the strap so it comes away from her hipbone.

I knew what he wanted.

My submission. My willingness to do what he asked.

No questions. No fighting.

I could feel the numbness seep in at the edges to begin with. There was no way I wasn't going to do what he asked. There was no question as to whether this was right. I'd save her.

"Yes."

His hand came away, "then you be a good little girl."

"She stays in here with me," I told him.

He laughs, "you are in no position to negotiate, daughter."

"Then I'll scream and I'll scream. Kill us both. Do it, you coward."

His nostrils flared.

"I'll fight. I'll make sure I do everything I can to stop whatever it is you have planned. I don't believe you won't harm her the moment my door is closed, the only way I will behave is if she stays in here with me."

Marcus growled, grabbed Rory and launched her across the room, causing her body to slam into the wall with a hard thud. With a whimper she sunk down to the floor.

There were no more words. No more threats. They untied me and pushed me back towards the bed before leaving and bolting the door behind them.

I didn't waste a second. I moved to where Rory lay crumbled on the floor and gathered her into my arms.

The only way I could save her was by sacrificing myself and the only way I'd ever be able to comply with my fathers wishes was to become a shell. To become nothing.

"I'm so sorry Wren," Aurora sobbed, "I'm so sorry." But she had nothing to be sorry for, this was my fault.

I smoothed my hand down her dried and dirty hair, trying to soothe her and when she stopped crying, I guided her to the bed, gently nudging her into it.

"Sleep," I told her, "You're safe here."

She may have been safe with me but what will happen when I eventually leave? Marcus wasn't planning on keeping me here, I knew that much at least, when I was gone who would look after her?

If I didn't do something she'd die down here.

I come back to the present, eyes flicking to the top of the bed where she sits with her legs pulled up to her chest, still in that blue dress. Her eyes are wide, full of fear as she watches Valentine's men manhandle me. They tug a white dress over my head, forcing my arms into it roughly and pulling it down to cover my body though my wounds are hardly concealed.

When one of them wraps their beefy hand around my arm and yanks me to my feet, I let him, the pain in my body only reminding me I'm alive and nothing more. I'm not scared. I don't fear what is going to happen next.

I don't allow thoughts of Lex.

I only think about the girl behind me and how doing this stops her pain.

I follow, like the little willing captive up the stairs to the warmth of the house and further through to a den like room where I'm positioned in the corner of an office.

And that's where I wait to learn what's to happen to me next.

10

Wren

I'm standing for what feels like hours, my legs ache from the prolonged position and I'm growing tired. The room is too warm, and the scent of cigar smoke and whiskey tinges the air. Marcus sits behind a giant desk, clearly trying to compensate for *something* with his fingernail tapping incessantly on the hardwood. Two guards stand at the doorway, staring straight ahead at the wall behind Marcus' head like the good little dogs they are.

A radio crackles and then a raspy voice sounds through the speaker.

"He's here, over."

Marcus stands abruptly and smooths his hands down the lapels of his dark suit jacket, tugging at the collar to straighten it out. He fidgets with the cufflinks and then pats at the weapon he has tucked into a holster at his back. He's nervous which means whoever is about to enter is clearly more dangerous than this man.

That should scare me. It doesn't.

His eyes dart to me and he curls his lip as if what I have to offer is less than favorable.

Whatever.

He did this to me.

"Stand up straight," he barks.

With a roll of my eyes, I do as he asks and link my fingers together in front of me, hiding the twitch.

The door to the den opens and a flurry of activity happens, men dressed nothing like the ones in this house file into the room. These guys look casual in dark jeans, dark tees and leather jackets or hoodies. They're tattooed, rough around the edges but the air around them crackles with power. They're not people to be messed with. It's completely silent until the final man steps into the room and finally, *finally,* my body reacts. Fear makes my heart pound harder, makes my palms sweat and causes my throat to become dry. It's hard to swallow, a lump the size of a golf ball now sitting there. I peel my tongue from the roof of my mouth, my blood roaring in my ears as my heart thumps wildly.

He's dressed like the rest, in a pair of dark jeans but he wears a white tee and no jacket. Dark tattoos cover both arms, from his fingers all the way up until they disappear under the cuffs of his t-shirt. They snake up his neck, there's even a small one on the side of his head, barely visible with the short dark hair growing over it.

His eyes are the lightest shade of blue I've ever seen, like the Caribbean sea with the sun bouncing off the calm waters. His sharp, stubbled jaw is clamped tight, the muscles in his cheeks jumping with each grind of his teeth. A straight nose with a piercing in one nostril and lips, full and far too soft looking for a man like him are pressed into a flat line. To look at directly, you wouldn't say he was a huge man, not when compared to the beefcakes Marcus employs or even against Lex and Ryker but he was athletically built, toned and lithe. His clothes fit him perfectly, outlining the hard lines of his abdomen. He surveys the room, first looking at Valentine's men, and then at Valentine. A quick appraisal later and those eyes made of ice land on me. He surveys me from the top of my head to the tips of my toes. He narrows his eyes each time he comes across a bruise or cut, and I can't help but squirm under that penetrating gaze.

I don't feel like I'm in danger when he looks at me. No hostility, no imminent threat which probably means I really am fucked, well and truly.

"Mr Heart," Marcus steps forward, towards the man he's just referred to as Mr Heart and his gaze snaps away from me back to my father.

"Don't," Heart growls, his English accent strong, sophisticated, curling his lip and stopping Marcus in his tracks, his arm still outstretched ready to shake his hand.

"Kingston," a melodic feminine voice scolds softly and I look behind him to see a woman stepping in behind him.

Kingston's nostrils flare and his hands ball into fists at his sides. He doesn't seem pissed that she's just interrupted him, if anything his whole demeanor has just switched from killer to protector. The woman comes up next to him, close but not so close it says intimacy and I study the newcomer.

She's gorgeous. Long, black hair falls around her face like silk, the lights in the room bouncing off the tresses and her skin is flawless but incredibly pale. Her eyes are the same color as Kingston's, a blue so icy they freeze everything they touch and her pouty, full lips are painted blood red. She has a snow white vibe about her if snow white had all the lethal grace of a lioness.

She's lithe like the man beside her, tall with a slender yet toned frame, dressed in skin tight black jeans and a white blouse that flows over her torso and a pair of black boots with heels that if I wore I'd likely break an ankle.

She doesn't survey the room like Kingston did, instead her eyes home in on me instantly and soften. Surely that can't be right. Why would they be softening?

"Marcus," Kingston grumbles reluctantly, "This is my sister, Isobel."

Marcus appears to like Isobel very much if the way he's devouring her with his eyes is anything to go by. His tongue may as well be hanging out of his face.

A few of Kingston's men step closer to the lone female in their group, shoulders squaring, a warning to Valentine to back the fuck up.

I'd laugh if I could.

"You did not mention you'd be bringing a female," Marcus drags his gaze away from the woman and lands back on Kingston.

I can't gage him. Is he friend of foe?

I scoff internally. Of course he's foe. Look at him.

There may as well be a neon light flashing above his head that reads DANGER in big bright letters.

"Is that a problem?" Kingston's mouth tips up at the edge, a smirk knowing Marcus will never admit that he doesn't think women belong on the same level as men.

"Not at all."

I can't stifle the laugh.

The slap across the face is quick and painful. I didn't even see him cross the room until his hand was striking me. The pain burns in my cheekbone and unable to control my basic instincts, I lash out, though I don't get far. Not even a finger to his skin as he steps back to a safe distance and one of his men restrains me.

Marcus glares at me, promising me punishment for that later.

Fuck.

When I look back to the Heart siblings all I see is amusement. Isobel watches me with so much glee you'd think she was a kid on Christmas and Kingston peruses me with an air of respect.

"You're Alexander Silver's woman, are you not?" He asks me directly.

"She's nothing." Marcus snaps.

"Was I speaking with you?" Kingston doesn't even turn to look at Valentine, keeping his icy gaze on me, urging me to talk.

Swallowing, I nod, "I was."

"Was?"

"I hardly think I belong to him now."

Kingston laughs, "Oh you belong to him alright. It's nice to finally meet the woman who brought the king to his knees."

I don't sense malice in his words, and it just confuses me more. Kingston Heart was an enigma.

He turns back to Valentine, "Brave of you to mess with a Silver, Valentine, what makes you believe I'd also want to fuck with that family? You do know who they are, yes?"

"We had a deal," Marcus sputters.

"Now, now, Valentine," Kingston chuckles, "don't get ahead of yourself. I never said anything about backing out of the deal. I just want to make sure you understand what you have gotten yourself into."

"I am aware," Marcus growls, "Now, do you want her or not? If not, I have a list of buyers more than willing to take her in exchange for resource."

"Ah," Kingston holds up a finger, "but none with resources like mine, right?"

Marcus glowers, "no."

Whilst the men are talking Isobel has edged closer, so close in fact she's standing directly in front of me.

Marcus has taken notice, "Is she for you or your sister?" The slimy smile that drags up his mouth is nauseating.

Isobel sneers in his direction but keeps her eyes trained on me, cautiously lifting her hand to whisper her fingers over the blooming bruise on my cheek. Her face is soft, almost kind as her eyes drop down my body. "What did he do to you?" She whispers.

I swallow and frown. What the fuck is going on here?

"I'll take her and I'll give you want you want," Kingston confirms, forcing me to look away from his sister to the man himself. I was being sold. Like fucking livestock.

"I'll make your life hell," I warn him.

Kingston smirks, "I hope you do."

Isobel gently grips my arm and begins to drag me towards her brother.

She's suddenly stopped by one of Valentine's men who snatches her arm, pulling her roughly towards him.

The sounds of guns being withdrawn and safety catches being switched off has my spine straightening.

Kingston has a gun directly aimed at Marcus whilst Marcus has one pointed at Isobel and me.

Well fuck.

"You don't take the woman until I have what I want." Marcus barks.

"I think you're severely outnumbered here, Valentine. I'll kill you and your men in three seconds flat. You think we're the only ones on this property right now?"

Marcus' eyes widen a fraction but he stifles it down quickly, "And I'll kill your precious little Isobel."

Kingston's nostrils flare as he cocks his head, "Belle, let go of the girl. We'll be back for her."

"But –" Isobel starts.

"Now, Isobel."

She lets go gently and sighs heavily before joining her brother, the gun following her the entire time.

"I'll have what you need brought to you by tomorrow night. I don't want a hand on her."

Marcus cocks a brow, "She still belongs to me until you

deliver, Kingston, I'll do as I please until then, if you don't want her touched you best make the delivery quick."

Big words for a man who trembles in this guys presence. But it's all about looks and they can be awfully deceiving.

Kingston's smile is cruel, "Let's go," he orders his guys before his eyes bounce to mine, "We'll be seeing each other again real soon."

11

Lex

"Where?" My hand slams down on the table.

I had enemies coming out my fucking ears, everywhere I turned there was someone, another fucker trying to take over my kingdom. Take what belonged to me.

Kingston fucking Heart was in my city.

I'd never met the bloke but I've heard enough and I needed him gone before he could cause too much fucking stink in these streets.

Why was he even here? What the fuck could Brookeshill have that he wants.

I wasn't scared of the guy but I wasn't stupid either. The biggest underground organization in Europe with ties *everywhere.* Kingston Heart and his sister were nightmares whispered on the wind and it didn't matter which side of the line you were on, if you got in their way you'd be crushed before you could even blink. They made a lasting impression wherever they stepped. There was a reason I didn't associate with the likes of them, I may be strong, and I may have this fucking city, everyone in it and my resources and contacts may be vast, but they were a whole other level.

And they were in my fucking city.

"Spotted down on the northside docks," Ryker grunts, swiping through the image surveillance we had managed to get, "they weren't doing shit though. Just standing there."

I look down at the images. There are fucking hundreds of them here. To look at, Kingston didn't appear to be much, a little menacing but that was it, but I knew better than to believe he was harmless. Oh no, that man made even the devil shake.

It was possible that him and I could have gotten along at some point, but not now. Not now that he has stormed my city uninvited.

"Does anyone know where they were before that?" I ask, swiping through more images. Kingston lazes against the barrier, drawing in from a cigarette whilst his sister talks on the phone. Even though I've never met them in person, I know damn well out of the two of them, Isobel is the most unhinged. Fucking batshit actually. The stories, Jesus Christ, the fucking stories of the men she's strung up using nothing but their fucking balls and the tales of their DIY castrations.

Most of their life is private, where and how they were raised, their parents, all of it. One minute they weren't there and the next they were fucking everywhere, taking over Europe like a plague.

I had to respect them at least.

Ryker shakes his head, tapping the images with the tip of his finger, "Before this they hadn't been seen. Do you not think that strange?"

It wasn't merely a coincidence that they were here. With Valentine and the Syndicate breathing poison into my city, there was no way they were simply here for a vacation. They had a part in this but where, I didn't know. Could they have been the English Jameson mentioned before he died?

I flick to another image and stop dead. Kingston is staring directly at the camera, one brow cocked and a smirk on his face. In the next picture he's holding up nine fingers.

What the fuck.

What the hell does the number nine have to do with this.

After that image it's just a picture of him checking his watch and then rounding up his guys, heading towards a convoy of dark SUVs. They headed out the city and haven't returned since. That was early this morning and it's now eight the same evening.

I press my fingers to the bridge of my nose.

Valentine hasn't sent any more images of Wren. I've had nothing since the last one and his men have disappeared off the streets. All the hideouts we've found them at previously are empty. Everyone has just fucking vanished.

I'd take that as a good sign usually but not this time round, not when my little bird is still missing and Valentine is still trying to take the city.

Now with the Heart's here, I know it's all connected.

But how?

Fuck I hated not being in control.

It made me crazy.

She made me crazy.

I had her at my side and it turned my whole world upside down and now she's not there, everything I've ever known doesn't make any sense. The only thing that matters now is getting her back. I'll pile the bodies and I'll stain the streets until she's here. Where she belongs.

My phone buzzes in my pocket and I pull it out to see an unknown number calling.

"Silver," I answer.

"Son," my fathers voice crackles through the speaker.

My anger spikes, "How nice of you to finally reach out," I growl.

"Go to the study," he orders, ignoring my tone.

I comply as much as I don't want to, walking away from Ryker who still studies the images in front of him, trying to piece together Heart's movements.

"You're making an awful lot of noise," my father tells me after I've locked the door and taken a seat at the desk, pouring two fingers of scotch into my glass.

"Yes well, people are fucking with things that do not belong to them."

"We're not talking about the city," it isn't a question, a statement which I do not deny. "All of this for a woman."

Again, I say nothing because there is nothing to say.

"She better be fucking worth it, Alexander. I didn't raise a bitch."

"Ha," I laugh without humor, "Not that I need to justify my actions old man, this is my kingdom now, but she is worth it."

"Good. Then you need to know that the Syndicate are in your ranks."

I had my suspicions. I didn't know who or how but they were here.

"I know."

"I can't say much, Alexander, I'm being monitored to

see how much I know but they are deeming this old man useless now I'm not in the city."

"Who are they exactly?"

"The Syndicate have been around longer than even the Silvers, a small organization initially but they amassed a following. They're a parasite, coming in and killing off the hosts before taking over the body. They want the world. They do it silently but I've been watching them for some time."

"And you didn't think to warn me of this?"

"I didn't think they'd come for Brookeshill so soon."

"Wonderful."

"Like all things Lex, they have a weakness. They live for their anonymity, they're businessmen, by day they're like any other fucker on the street, they have wives and children, day jobs but by night they're killers and thieves and scum. They want power and money and they'll go to any lengths to get it. Drugs. Humans, you name it, they'll do it."

"Fuck."

"They don't live by the same rules as we do, son. Nothing is off limits. There are no laws, no moral code, they take and take and they'll use any means to get it. Stand in their way or cause a problem for them they'll take out the issue. Like your little girlfriend."

"Why get Valentine to do their dirty work?"

"Valentine was an easy pawn to them, he was hungry for your throne and whilst they'll do anything to take what they want they don't like getting their hands dirty. They know they can't simply take you out without losing the city and the loyalty, if Valentine does it for them and claims the city, your men will either die with you or swear new loyalty to him if they want to keep the money rolling. It's war, Lex."

"You should have warned me," I growl.

"I'm warning you now." He says, "take them out. All of them."

"I'm fucking trying!"

"Five five five, south street, it's a safe house only I know about. When –" *not if,* "you get your woman back, put her there until this is over. She's your weakness Lex, and they'll use it. Hide her."

Silence settles between us.

"I understand."

There is no goodbye as he hangs up and for a moment I sit in the quiet, sipping my whiskey.

But I should have known the quiet wouldn't last. It never fucking does.

The alarm sounds on my phone just as Ryker bursts through the door, "We've got company."

12

Two hours earlier

Despite his threat, Valentine didn't lay a finger on me. I was shoved back into the room minutes after Kingston and his men left and I've been here ever since. Rory is doing better, her wounds now healing but her mind still needs to be fixed. It's too often I find her staring at the wall, her eyes filled with horror as she remembers all that she's endured since she's been here.

She wakes often, screaming and lashing out and those nightmares trickle into her waking hours. I don't know if she'll ever be the same again.

"What did he do?" She asked an hour after I was put back.

I shake my head, not wanting to tell her I'll be leaving. I didn't want to think about what they would do with her when I was gone, and I was trying to think of ways of either negotiating her release or convincing Kingston to take her with us. It was obvious he wouldn't allow it, this wasn't a package deal, whatever he was trading with my father made him as bad as everyone else. He came here because he wanted me. No-one could be trusted.

The door opens a crack and two sealed bottles of water are rolled in before the door slams shut once more. I grab them and throw one over to my best friend, breaking the seal on mine and taking a sip.

"How did you end up here?" I ask instead.

She looks down at her hands, "I don't really know. It was a few weeks ago I guess, I'm not actually sure how long it's been but I was coming out of school, it was quite late because I was grading, when someone hit me. When I woke up, I was in that room down the hall."

She sniffles.

"Don't tell me the rest, Rory, I don't need to know that."

"They hurt me," she whispers. "Real bad."

"I know," I cross the room to sit next to her, "I'm going to get us out of here."

It's amusing comparing this experience to the one with Lex, I'm determined to get out of here, but where was that determination when I was strapped to Lex's bed.

I lift my water bottle to my lips, but a sudden boom causes me to flinch, making me drop the open bottle onto the floor. The walls shake and the ceiling above me vibrates, dislodging dust and dirt that rains down onto us. Another boom has all the lights going out and with the fact that we're underground and there's no windows the room plunges into a darkness so deep I can't see my hand in front of my face.

Rory screams next to me, snatching out to wrap her dainty fingers around my arm painfully, her nails digging into my skin.

There are a few beats of silence before the sound of gunfire comes. The loud pops make my ears ring and the shouts and hollers coming from above leaves my brain scrambling to keep up. Feet pound against the floorboards above us, frantic, panicked and the gun fire continues.

I pry Rory's fingers from my arm as I climb from the bed, my bare feet scuffing across the floor. A door slams close by and then footsteps are drawing closer quickly. Before I can react the door to the room swings open, letting in a tiny amount of light from the emergency lighting I hadn't realized had been installed into the ceilings of this underground prison. Marcus's face is shrouded in menacing shadows and the gleam of a knife catches in the dim light. He lunges forward, slicing the knife into my flesh. I manage to dodge but it still cuts through my skin, just below my ribs, deep enough for a well of blood to pour down my side and hip, staining the white dress crimson. I cry out as he grabs my throat having dropped the knife in our scuffle.

"No one gets you!" He growls. "No one fucking gets you!"

I try to frantically suck in air as his palms crush my windpipe, all the while Rory screams, her fists slamming into Marcus's back but it's useless. She's too weak to fight him off and me, I'm losing too much blood too quickly.

Fuck.

"Get off!" Rory cries. "Get off!"

A door slamming has Valentine's hands loosening and then they come away entirely as he spins and runs.

Runs.

The fucking coward.

I collapse onto my knees, sucking in breaths as my blurring vision follows his dark shape out the door. I blink once, twice, staring at my freedom. The door is open. We can get out.

I clutch Rory's hand, pushing onto shaky legs as I clutch my side, trying to stem the bleeding.

I should be dead. I will be if I can't stop myself from bleeding out.

If I die though, I will be out of this house. Even if that death happens on the front porch, I'll be free and so will Rory.

I make a step towards the door and that sense of freedom dies as a body fills the doorframe.

"Hello, Wren," Kingston's smooth English accent sends a warning shiver down my spine.

Will someone give me a fucking break!?

Men run behind him, opening doors, the metal clanging of keys loud as it echoes through the halls. There's still the odd pop of gun fire up above but it's obvious Kingston is the winner here.

"You're hurt," he comments, with a cock of his head as his eyes drop to the blood seeping through my fingers, "I don't think Silver will be best pleased with me bringing you back broken."

Confusion has my head snapping back, "W-what did you say?"

"Let's go, Wren," he curls his fingers, beckoning me forward.

It may be fucking stupid, real dumb but I go, grabbing Rory as my weak legs carry me towards the man that I have no doubt has been the star of many a nightmare.

When I get to him, my legs give out but he doesn't let me hit the floor, no, his arms snatch out, grabbing me before I can break my nose on the concrete.

"Not pleased at all," he tuts, mostly to himself as I'm dragged back into a standing position and hoisted up. Fog clouds my mind, coming in heavy at the edges but I can tell I'm moving, or maybe I'm floating.

"Don't you die on me, love," Kingston says, "I need

you alive and kicking."

"You're going to use me too," my voice is weak, small.

"It's more of a peace offering," he tells me.

"W-why?"

"Your man has a lot of power, I'll be stupid to get on the wrong side of him but I need his help."

"You're taking me to Lex?"

"I am, love, now stay alive," he orders, "I hate it when people die on me, especially since I've gone to all this trouble."

"Rory…" my voice trails off.

"All the girls here will be taken care of," Kingston says.

I know the moment we step outside.

Cool air washes over my feverish skin and even in my current state it lights something inside of me. My lungs expand as I suck in the fresh air, feeling the wind on my face, teasing through my limp and unwashed hair. Freedom.

I'm free.

A numbness begins to spread through my body as Kingston continues to carry me away from the house but I don't fight it. I'm not going to die inside that house, inside that prison. I'm not going to be left to rot in a

ditch. I'm free. I feel myself being lowered, the pain in
my side a dull throb compared to the fog inside my head.

 "There goes the car seats," a feminine voice chimes
from somewhere in front of me.

 "Shut it, Belle," Kingston orders, climbing into the back
with me, "drive. Now."

 The movement of the car has my stomach rolling and I
gag though nothing comes up and then my eyes roll
back, my consciousness slipping.

 "Oh no you don't," Kingston shakes me roughly as he
presses something into my side, "What did I say, love?
Stay alive."

 But that shit was easier said than done when all I
wanted to do was sleep.

13

Present

I grab my gun from the holster at my back and then snatch the other from where I've attached it under the desk, my legs pounding against the floor as I dart out of the office, towards the front of the house.

Oh, we had company alright.

There was a small fucking army in the compound grounds. The gates at the front of the house didn't fucking stand a chance against the convoy of SUVs barrelling down my driveway.

Fuck.

Heart was here and he was making his presence known.

"Hold your fire!" Someone booms from outside, a body

stepping from the closest vehicle with their hands raised.

"It's a trap," Ryker hisses.

"Hold your fire," I growl out the order.

"Where is Silver!?" The English accent has my eyes narrowing though it isn't Heart shouting towards us but one of his men.

One of my guys raises his pistol, "Hold it for fucks sake," I hiss, unfolding my body until I'm standing. Ryker rises with me, I can see it in his face that he thinks this is a bad idea and I don't know why, call it intuition, but something is pulling me towards the door.

I open it, my gun still in hand and raised, ready to fire but I don't pull the trigger.

When the guy spots me he lowers his weapon and steps to the side, nodding his head once.

Heart steps from the vehicle but it isn't him I'm interested in.

Oh no.

It's the broken body he has cradled in his arms that has me moving.

My little bird.

The threat, the dangerous, very real possibility of having a bullet between the eyes in the next three seconds is lost on me as I cross the space, the gravel crunching under my feet until I'm directly in front of Kingston Heart. Blood coats his hands, his forearms, the front of his t-shirt but he doesn't matter as he simply hands the girl to me. Her body is too cold, too thin, too *still*. There's too much blood. Too many cuts and bruises. Her chest barely moves with the shallow breaths that she inhales through slightly parted pale lips. Dying. She was dying.

"A doctor!" I boom, "Now!" Crippling fear takes a vice like grip around my heart.

There's a flurry of movement behind me.

"If a doctor isn't here in ten minutes, I'll kill you all," I stare at every face I can see, the promise of my words penetrating deep inside their brains. I would do it. For her, I'd kill them all.

To my surprise, Heart lets me leave but he, his sister and a few of his men follow. I wasn't going to stop him.

I owed him.

He did this for a something in return, there's no way a man like him, so much like myself did this out of the kindness of his heart.

There is no compassion in his soul. Strategy. Ruthlessness. Intelligence. All of them but never compassion.

He's king where he comes from like I'm king here.

Having Wren back in my arms feels like I've come

home. It's a sense that burrows deep into my soul, swelling my chest until I feel as if my lungs and heart will burst right out. It's not a feeling I'm used to.

It fucking terrifies me.

Upstairs, in the master bedroom, I gently lay her onto the bed, placing her head on the pillow so her hair fans out around her head like a halo of fire. It's not glossy or wild like it usually is, just limp, weak.

Her pouty mouth is pressed into a thin line and her skin is almost translucent beneath the lights in the bedroom. The prominent bones of her collar and ribs protrude from her skin like sharp edges.

"Get out!" I bark at the men that followed me in and all but Ryker leave, clicking the door closed.

"Kingston Heart is downstairs, Lex," he warns.

"Do I look like I give a shit?"

"Lex," Ryker starts.

"Get the fuck out!"

Ryker stops in his tracks as he makes his way towards me and Wren. Panic has started to crawl through my body, it makes my scalp tingle, my palms sweat.

This much emotion I can't control. "GET OUT!"

"Lex," Ryker tries again, fucking pushing, always fucking pushing.

106

A loud crash echoes through the house which distracts us for a moment, "I'll deal with it."

My nostrils flare, "you do that."

When I'm finally alone, when silence settles like a heavy weight around me, I sit on the bed, pulling my broken bird into me, resting her head in my lap, smoothing back the hair from her face.

"You left me little bird," I whisper, "you fucking left me."

Her lips part and her lashes flutter but she doesn't open her eyes.

"I'm going to make him pay for this, mark my words little bird, you'll be standing at my side whilst we watch his heart beat in my fist. I'll make it rain, little bird. For you. Always for you."

"Lex," her voice is as soft as a summer breeze, "Alexander."

"I'm here."

A small whimper escapes her lips as her body shivers against me and a single tear slips out the corner of her eye, rolling down the side of her face to disappear into her copper hairline. Her breathing is still too shallow, her breaths slow.

I hate seeing her like this. No fight. No strength. As much as I fucking loathed her attitude and her push, I wished for it now. I needed her venom if only to teach her a lesson, I needed her fight and her strength if only to prove I'd always own her, always have her.

I wanted to both devour and soothe her broken frame, to love her and worship her whilst I claimed her. Made her mine.

I'd ensure the whole fucking world knew she belonged to a Silver and fucking with her was fucking with an army bigger, better and stronger than any of our enemies.

I'd make her a Silver, have her at my side, a crown atop her head and make them all bow down. They'll bend the knee and kiss her feet like she fucking deserved.

The doctor arrives seven minutes after the threat, sweating, his eyes wide with fear, his equipment tugged in behind him by the nurses he's no doubt managed to blackmail onto his payroll.

Doctor Gerald Whitmore was a seedy old man but a good doctor, he's patched me up many a time and I had no doubt Wren was in capable hands.

"Mr Silver," he greets, swallowing nervously.

"Fix it."

"You know that is not how this works, Mr Silver," he steps towards us and instinctively, I bend, covering my woman, baring my teeth like a fucking animal.

"You'll need to let him at her," a strong English accent says from the door.

"Heart," I growl.

"In the flesh," his arms stretch out at his sides, palms facing towards the ceiling, "She took a beating Silver, you want her to live, the good doctor is gonna need to see her."

He's right. I fucking hate it.

Reluctantly, I uncurl myself from her and retract enough to let Whitmore in. He tugs at her clothes, pulling the fabric away from her skin and the urge to protect makes not ripping his throat out almost impossible.

"Look at me, Silver," Heart drawls, "stop picturing all the ways you could disembowel the doctor."

Whitmore audibly swallows.

"What the fuck do you want?"

I allow the distraction, trying to ignore the doctors hands on Wren's body. She needs this. She needs to live. To breathe. To survive and the only way that is happening is with him.

"To talk, Silver."

"You've come all the way from London to talk?" I scoff.

"Amongst other things," Kingston nods, "now isn't a good time but I'm not going anywhere."

"And what's stopping me putting a knife through your

throat?"

Kingston smirks, eyes bouncing to my woman, now half naked and bleeding across my sheets. A growl leaves my throat. The only warning I'll give.

"You're a man of code, Silver. I gave you something and you don't like debt."

"And I don't like fuckers walking in on my turf, regardless of whether you've done something for me."

Kingston nods slowly, "I get that but unfortunately for you, I don't give a shit. We need to talk, don't make this harder than it has to be."

I have too much going on to pick a fight with a man who owns half of Europe and despite the fact that he's busted in on my fucking turf, I did owe him for bringing me Wren.

"Fine, now leave. We'll talk when I'm ready."

I don't wait to see if he accepts that, just turn back to my girl. My eyes fall to the healing wound in the centre of her abdomen, the healing scar where the bullet ripped through her skin. There are old and new cuts all over her, dark and fading bruises and the wrapped thigh with blood spots staining the white makes my blood fucking boil.

"I'll be here a while," the doc says.

And so I wait. I settle into the chair across from the bed and wait whilst the doc fixes up my woman, unable to focus on anything other than her. All the problems, they'll still be here tomorrow but there's not a guarantee she will be.

Wren

I hear his voice. A deep soothing baritone that both scares and excites me. It's the type of noise that brings a surge of memories to the surface, his hands on my body, his tongue on my skin, teeth grazing, nails biting. It isn't real. It can't be.

I'm in hell.

But the memories, they keep torturing me as his breath brushes my ear, the smell of whiskey on the air. His possessive growl, his ruthlessness, his violence, his demons. They caress my body like hands, making me *feel*. I don't want to feel. I can't. Not in this life.

If I feel, I'll die and Rory won't ever be free.

"I've been looking for you, little bird," his growl is barely audible, a whisper in the darkness, taunting me, "You left me, but I came looking. I'll always come looking."

The absolute sorrow that overtakes me in this moment is crippling. Why am I being tortured with thoughts of Lex? Why is it him haunting me?

The sob echoes in the darkness and for the first time, everything hurts. My head, my body, my heart. All of me is on fire as agony rips through me.

And as if to haunt me more, as if I haven't suffered enough strong arms band around me, gently, barely even touching my skin but there nonetheless and a mouth is pressed to my hair.

"Shh, I've got you, little bird," are his whispered words. "Shh now, that's it. Good girl."

But whilst I quiet, the pain continues, eating away at my soul. I'm left to the demons and the nightmares whilst I hallucinate Alexander by my side.

14

Something isn't right. It isn't the smell of coffee or the
voices in the room with me, it isn't the familiar scent of
Lex's aftershave or the soft sheets beneath my body, it's
the steady presence at my back. The soft hand on my
body, the feel of another person breathing behind me, the
steady rise and fall of their chest pressing into my spine.

No.

This isn't right. My eyelids feel heavy as I try to open
them, the burning light coming in through a window
right in front of me scolding my retinas. What the fuck?
There's a window? Daylight and trees and grass.

I curl my fingers, feeling the soft cotton yield under my
grip and squint, trying to get a look of the room without
notifying anyone around me that I'm awake. My skin
feels too tight for my bones and my throat is dry, but I
don't dare move or make a sound. The walls are white
with a pair of navy curtains hanging at the window, the
bedside table is one I recognize, dark colored with a
lamp on the top and drawers. Everything is so similar. Is

this just another way for Valentine to torture me? Give me what I want only to burn it to the ground later.

Footsteps sound, heading away from me and then a door is closed, the soft click making me jump where I lay, still with that body pressed behind me.

A few beats of silence where the only sound in the room is my frantic breathing but then that rough voice is whispering against my ear, the hint of mint brushing against my nose.

"I know you're awake, little bird."

My heart stops beating, the breath ceasing to continue as I push away from where I'm led on my side to position myself onto my back, it hurts and my skin pulls and twinges with the movement but nothing right now is going to stop me from seeing the face behind me.

I swallow as I start at his clothed legs, dressed in a pair of black suit trousers, his ankles crossed and then work my way up to where his black shirt is tucked into the pants, a black belt with a silver buckle holding it together. I follow the line of the buttons before they stop, creating a V to reveal the hard expanse of his chest, prominently lined muscles and bronzed skin, and then further up his throat, noticing the way his Adam's apple bobs as he swallows. The hard line of his jaw twitches as he grits his teeth and then I see his mouth.

His beautiful, dangerous mouth, set in a straight line.

When I meet his eyes the whole world stops. Silver orbs bore down into me, filled with so much emotion it gives

114

me whiplash. I've never seen him reveal so much in his face, but it's there, as if it's typed into his skin with ink. Pain. Regret. Fear.

His eyes bounce between mine, but this can't be real, can it?

His dark hair is slicked back away from his face, but one tendril falls across his forehead which creases with a frown as he looks at me.

Is this a dream? Am I dreaming?

His finger comes up to caress the side of my face, the very tip, following the line of my cheek, across my jaw until it brushes over my bottom lip.

"Lex?"

One side of his mouth tips up, "Hello, Little Bird."

Fuck the pain. Fuck the obvious injuries, I scramble, trying to get to my knees but his firm hand holds me down, pinning me in place.

"Let me up!"

This earns me a grin as he flips himself, getting to his knees, the mattress dipping beneath his weight. He cages me between his arms, face hovering above mine.

"I've missed you little bird and I've never missed anything in my entire life."

"Kiss me damn it!"

His eyes bounce between mine but whatever he was
looking for he must find because his mouth crashes
down on mine possessively. His hands may be gentle, he
may be holding himself away from my body but his
mouth is not in any way soft as his tongue pushes in
through my lips. Fuck he tastes good.

It's been too long.

I never thought I'd miss the man, I didn't even think I'd
ever need a man, but I needed him. I needed him as
much as I needed air to fill my lungs. We're inexplicably
linked, his demons and his darkness caressed my soul.

He rips himself away, practically throwing himself off
the bed to get away from me, but I just lay there. Part of
me believes this is still a dream, still a nightmare but my
swollen lips, the wetness there transferring to my
fingertips as I brush my fingers across my mouth seem
all too real.

I find him breathing heavy at the edge of the bed,
"Don't do that again."

"What?"

"You're injured, Wren, this," he points between us,
"This ain't happening."

"Are you fucking kidding me?"

His eyes narrow, "Just because you're incapacitated
right now doesn't mean I won't put you over my knee
the moment you're less *fragile*."

116

"Don't make promises you can't keep."

He grins, his white teeth almost gleaming when compared to the bronze tone of his skin. Goddamn he's so fucking beautiful.

I try to push up onto my elbows but the pain in my side cripples me. I cry out, squeezing my eyes shut as my blood roars. Fuck, that hurts.

How the fuck did I even get here? I remember the loud bang, Valentine attacking me and then Kingston. After that, I don't remember a single thing.

Oh God. Rory!

Ignoring the pain, the agony that wants to pull me under, I get up onto shaky legs, pushing away the blankets. There's no time to think about the fact that I'm dressed in a pair of leggings and a t-shirt that's three times too big for me. Where is Rory?

"Stop!" Lex booms.

Had he been talking? I'm halfway to the door but I stop, my knees shaking, threatening to buckle under me.

"Where the fuck do you think you're going?"

Lex appears in front of me, his nostrils flaring, anger palpable.

"I just got you back little bird and you're trying to run away already?"

"No," I swallow, "no, you don't understand."

He steps up and curls a finger beneath my chin, "Tell me." My eyes meet his, swarming with emotion, with something far too deep for my mind to comprehend.

"My friend, Valentine, he had her and…"

"Shh," He brings me to his chest, "She's safe. All the girls are."

"Where?"

"Not now, Wren, you need to rest."

"Alexander," I grit out.

"Fight me, Wren, I dare you."

I didn't have the energy to fight him. Not even with words, as much as I wanted to lash out, to demand to know where she was I couldn't. I was so tired. In so much pain.

"What happened?"

He guides me back to the bed just as Ryker comes into the room with a bowl of soup and a couple of bottles of water.

"Good to see you awake," he comments, a gentle smile curling his lips.

"Hi Gruff." His eye roll makes me smile a little but it's the scent of the soup that really gets me going. My stomach gurgles loudly, cramping painfully, reminding me how little I've eaten in recent weeks.

He leaves the soup on the side, hands me a bottle of water and then exits whilst Lex settles into the bed next to me.

"So?"

I drink half the bottle of water whilst he just watches, head cocked to the side.

"Eat."

"Just tell me."

"Eat."

"You're so fucking bossy."

But I let him help me into a sitting position, trying to hide the wincing whilst he does, and then the tray is placed on my lap. He lowers the spoon, filling it with the red creamy liquid before lifting it and bringing it to my mouth. I open for him, letting him pour it into my mouth and onto my tongue. A groan sounds in the room. Lex smiles, his pupils dilating as he watches me eat, watching my mouth, my lips as they wrap around the spoon. I'm so taken by him and the food that I've eaten half the bowl before I realize it and come to my senses.

"Tell me, Lex."

With a sigh and the loud clang of the spoon hitting the side of the bowl, he explains the whole thing reluctantly.

Kingston and his sister, Isobel, belong to a huge organization based in Europe and whilst Lex doesn't know why he wants his help, the reason I'm here is because of him.

Kingston wants Lex so he used me to get to him.

I should feel angry that I'm simply a pawn, yet again, in a war that is not my own, but I just feel grateful towards the man.

Kingston helped bring me back.

I owed him.

But I also knew that debt wouldn't land on me, that's not how this world works. The debt is on Lex, it will always be on Lex until he pays it back. But I had no idea if whatever price Kingston was asking was going to be too high, even for the Twisted King of this city.

15

Lex

I watch Wren as she sleeps, still too fragile and pale for my liking. Cleaned and clothed now, she doesn't resemble the girl I lost in the club. There is something different about her. The trauma of what happened doesn't appear to have hit her yet but you don't go through what she did and come out of it with your mind in one piece. I am waiting for the time it hits.

I know it will. With an absolute certainty. She is not built for this, not yet anyway, she may be with time, but right now, she is still the same girl I took from her apartment all those weeks ago.

There are purple and blue bruises mottling her skin, too many cuts and grazes to count, swollen limbs and stitches with white bandages covering the wounds. She is lucky to be alive.

After eating plenty she fell into a quick sleep, exhausted but it was good to see a little fight in her.

I take the syringe of antibiotics and insert it into the

canular the doctor inserted into the top of her hand, administrating the medicine followed by a dose of painkillers that should keep her asleep for a little while. She'll hate me for it but I'll take it if it makes her better and keeps her safe.

Reluctantly, I slip from the room and close the door behind me, motioning for two of my guys to station themselves outside the door. I wasn't taking any chances. Keeping them here wasn't to keep her in the room, more to keep anyone who wasn't me *out.*

I take the stairs down quickly and find Ryker in the kitchen, his hands cradling a tumbler of whiskey whilst he hangs his head as if exhausted.

"What the fuck is wrong with you!?"

"That chick is batshit," he huffs, throwing back his drink.

He was referring to the blonde Kingston so lovingly deposited on my doorstep a few hours after bringing Wren to me.

Aurora Barrett.

If Kingston is to be believed, she went through some shit back at Valentine's compound, and the only reason she is alive is because of my little bird. Something I'll be having words with her for when she is well enough to hear them.

I knew the girl was important to Wren, you don't sacrifice yourself for someone you don't know but then

122

this is Wren, so fuck knows what she would do.

"Can't handle a little blonde?" I taunt, grabbing the bottle and pouring myself a drink before handing it back.

"She needs help." He says seriously.

"I don't have time for this shit," I growl at him, "I want Valentine's head."

"How is she?"

"Alive."

"Have you set up your meeting with Heart?"

"He's headed back to London for now but he'll be back next week," I sigh.

Whatever he wanted he was keeping it locked up tight. Kingston Heart, in his own right was a man not to be fucked with, he didn't scare me, not even a little but he had power. I recognized it, like for like, after all, recognize one and other.

It wasn't important right now. *She* was.

I've had men out, searching, tearing this city apart looking for Valentine or his men but it's like the man has disappeared yet again. The Syndicate are radio silent but this war is far from over.

Whilst Valentine licks his wounds the Syndicate are looking for another way to destroy my city.

No leads, no answers, no anything.

Everything was out of my control.

And I hated it.

I wanted blood.

I wanted pain.

I wanted vengeance.

A loud bang vibrates the ceiling above my head followed by loud yelling and grunts. Wren's friend was awake.

"Fuck," Ryker hisses, "how is she awake!? The doc gave her enough sedative to knock out a horse."

I didn't have the patience to deal with Aurora. I gave that shit to Ryker, if it were anyone else, I wouldn't give a fuck about her safety or health, I would have shoved her into the nearest hospital – *maybe* – and left it at that.

But I'd already determined that Wren was my weakness and I needed something to help bring Wren back when her mind can't handle the demons anymore.

I knew she was mine, she had admitted it but there is only so much I would be able to do. I may be a monster, evil, but my little bird was my tether and I would do anything for her.

Let it be said, even the devil can be tamed.

Ryker doesn't bother with a glass, he simply lifts the bottle from the table and swigs directly from it before shoving back from his chair and stomping from the room.

The call from my father rings in my head.

Five, five, five, south street.

A safe house.

Taking Wren there would be the safer option, but I wouldn't be able to stay. Not when the battle continues to rage on the streets. I wasn't sure if I'd be able to part with her now that I had her back. I throw the rest of my whiskey back and head back to the room. My men part to let me inside.

The room is shrouded in darkness, a small amount of silver light drifting in through the crack in the curtain but I see her shape writhing on the bed. Silently screaming as her dreams torture her in her sleep. So very broken.

Closing my eyes I try to settle the boiling rage before I cross the room and tug her into my lap, cradling her and restraining her to my chest to stop the thrashing. I can see speckles of blood seeping through the white bandages on her abdomen and her hair is slick with sweat but for whatever reason, be it pure insanity or not, she settles against me, the nightmares chased away by my presence.

Perhaps she was more broken than I thought.

Wren still sleeps when light streams in through the window the following morning. I worry about leaving her. I stare down at her face, tracing the lines of her nose, her cheeks, her perfectly shaped mouth with my eyes, unable to get enough.

Every emotion inside me feels too big, too important and I've no idea how to deal with or control them. I had always been taught that these feelings would be my destruction and now, as I stare at her, as everything inside me knots up so tightly I worry it'll snap, I understand why. This was nothing but obsession. I am *obsessed* with her. What the fuck do I do with that?

Gently, I pry her arm from my body and slip to the edge of the bed, running a hand down my face. Wren whimpers behind me but ultimately stays asleep as I drag my ass to the bathroom for a shower.

I have to harness this. Use it to my advantage. With how strongly I feel for my little bird it could bring some serious consequences, like seeing Valentine crucified on the tallest building of this city. He cannot hide for long, rats like him never go far and all I need to do is wait patiently for him to resurface.

I can do that.

I can wait.

Afterall, the sweetest meal comes to those who wait.

16·

Wren

I wake in a bath of golden sunlight, it streams in through the window, the curtains pulled back and a window open to let in a gentle breeze that caresses my overheated skin. My body hurts, bruises, and cuts and old wounds, pulsing with new and old pain that I fear will never go away.

A glance at the clock tells me it's a little past one in the afternoon but I have no idea what day it is. I don't know how long Marcus kept me locked in those cells beneath the house, how many days, weeks or even months passed before I was finally freed.

It's tough to remember everything, it's like since I've been back with Lex my mind has shut down on itself, as if, now it knows I am away from the imminent threat it can take a seat and turn off, no longer having to think too much in order to survive. I didn't blame it, part of me wanted to curl right back under this blanket and shut off.

Sitting up in bed, I stare around the room, the room I've shared with Lex on so many occasions but cannot remember the last before the blast. So much has happened, so much still happening and I can't work out my left from my right.

I run a hand down my face, frowning at the needle sticking out the back of my hand, strapped down with white medical tape.

My eyes narrow, I don't think so.

Ripping the tape off, I gently slide the needle out of my skin, watching as blood wells from the new hole in my hand. I press a hand to it to stop it from dripping everywhere and climb from the bed, heading across the room to the bathroom. Scents of Lex fill my nose, spicy and intoxicating, a familiar aroma that helps memories of his hands on my body fill the blank spaces inside my head.

There was one emotion pumping through my system, one feeling that kept my heart a steady thump inside my chest and that was having my revenge.

Lex might think he'll get to strike the final blow, but Marcus – *my father* – will die by my hand. He doesn't get to do this to me, *I will kill him.*

He has severely underestimated his own daughter and instead awoken something inside of me I feel has always been a part of my soul. A darkness that matches Alexander's. I always wondered why I felt attached to him somehow, always worried about why his breed of brutality spoke to me in ways I was never able to understand but now I know. And it's because I was born to be like him. To stand at his side. To rule and reign.

I stand before the mirror, in nothing but a tank top and a pair of white panties, all my wounds on show to me. The bruising on my throat, the shadows cast across my face from the number of hits and beatings I took at the hands of both Marcus and his men. At the gauze covering the slice in my side and another covering my thigh.

I stare at that one.

I can see dots of blood seeping through, staining the snow white bandage red but I can't remember what's under there. My head cocks to the side as I try to piece together the events that left me with this particular wound. What happened here?

I should probably leave it, but I have to shower anyway – *I really need to shower* – so unwrapping these bandages is a must.

I peel the tank top from my torso and do the one on my side first, keeping my eyes trained on the task rather than the scar that mars my abdomen from where I was shot. The wound in my side is still too raw to be left open but I can get away with it for an hour or so. I move to my thigh next, grabbing one end of the gauze, I start to unwrap it, taking each inch as slowly as possibly. My heart starts to pound furiously inside my chest, a sweat breaking out on my brow and between my breasts.

I know this is going to be bad. I already feel it, a sense of dread settling into the pit of my stomach as I continue to unroll the white material. Around and around it goes, only a few layers left before I can see what damage is lying underneath.

Finally, it falls away from my skin and drops to the floor, a puddle of white material mottled with red splotches.

Tears prick my eyes as I get a look at what that bastard did to me.

My own father.

I stare for the longest time, the tears welling in my eyes never spilling over, tracing the deep cut in my thigh, shaped in a V. He fucking branded me. Like livestock. Like cattle.

I am forever marked down as a Valentine. But I am not a Valentine.

I am a Silver.

Bile rises in my throat, a burn as my stomach churns, threatening to heave up anything that's in there though I doubt there will be much.

This can't stay. This needs to go.

Taking a deep breath, I meet my eyes in the mirror and realize what I must do.

Steeling myself, I nod and turn the shower on, letting the water heat to a near point of scolding before I step beneath the spray. It feels good, the water cascading over my overly sensitive skin, my muscles beginning to relax as the water soothes away the tension.

Other than the sound of the water, the bathroom is silent and even beyond that, I can't hear anything. It's in this moment the sounds of screams haunt my waking hours, shrieks of pure terror, of pain and suffering, it's the sounds of male grunts accompanied by the cries of the women they're torturing and the noise of blades and gunshots that fill the silence.

My knees are weak, too weak to keep me upright beneath the spray as these memories, memories that bounce around inside my head, one moment they are there, a pure vivid video replaying itself, the next they're gone, replaced by something else. Faces. Voices. Smells.

Rory.

Oh god. Rory.

Did she get out? Did I save her? Why can't I remember anything?

My sob is silent as I drop to my knees under the spray of the shower, the water hitting my spine, plastering my hair to my face. All my cuts stretch and pull as I move to sit under the spray, making me wince. Taking a deep breath, I try to calm my mind, try to push back the images to let in some light. Rory was safe. She got out.

Valentine did this.

He fucking did this.

I wanted to hold his heart in my hand. To watch the life

drain from him and I wanted to laugh and revel in it.

Everything up until this point has been a chain of events caused by him.

I wanted him to suffer.

The first thing I needed to do was get rid of this brand. It probably gives him joy to know that even if he doesn't have me, he still owns me in this way. His claws are in my skin and the only way to remove him is to remove this.

Sucking in a deep breath, I swipe at my face, closing my eyes to calm myself once more before I wash away the memories and turn off the shower.

Wrapping myself in a towel, I pick up the bloodied gauzes I left on the floor and shove them in the trash can just outside the bathroom door before I shut it and lock it behind myself. The mirror is steamed up, my reflection a blur of color in front of me but I don't need to see myself to do this.

I dry myself and stand there, on the cold tile floor in nothing, staring at the V carved right there into my thigh. It's still raw, not even knitted together properly yet, barely a scab. I close my eyes, the memory of how he did it slowly coming back to me, how he restrained me to a chair and carved into me with a knife. I remember his face, the twisted smile on his face, the look of pure joy in his eyes as that knife cut into my skin. He reveled in my pain just like I was going to revel in his.

I run my fingers over the wound, the flesh soft and

easily split as my nails scratch and disturb the dermis trying to grow over the top. I won't let it scar this way. I'd rather have a huge messy scar than the V carved into my thigh.

Lifting Lex's razor from the holder by the sink, I begin to pry the parts apart. First the handle, and then the casing that holds the blade in place. My fingers bleed from where the edge of the razor slices against my skin but I don't stop until the small little blade sits in my hand.

I stare at it for a while, this gleaming silver blade in the palm of my hand, used for nothing else but to shave the hair on Lex's face. But it's sharp and it'll do the job I need it to do.

In the time it has taken to dismantle the blade the mirror has cleared and I can see myself. I don't recognize the person that stares back at me. My red hair is slicked back from my face, dripping wet from the shower and leaving pools of water on the tiles beneath my feet, there are dark shadows under my eyes, even my freckles are dull and faded as if them too have simply given up. I'm too skinny, the bones of my collar and ribs protruding too far out of my skin, and my hip bones are sharp.

I lift my foot and rest the heel against the marble counter, remembering how I sat on that very counter, with Lex standing between my legs whilst I tended to *his* wounds. Swallowing, I line the blade against my thigh, but I don't intend to slice. Slicing won't get rid of the brand, I have to peel back this entire area to get rid of it. It'll leave me with one hell of a scar but rather that than this.

I grit my teeth and push, feeling my skin, still too sensitive, the nerves alive and exposed, peel away. I push, tears pricking my eyes with the pain as I push from the top of the V all the way down to the bottom, leaving a line of exposed flesh, bleeding and raw about ten centimeters long. Blood trickles from the new wound but I don't stop, I move to the next section, imbed the blade and push.

My teeth grit together, grinding inside my mouth loud enough to be heard.

Vaguely I am aware of a voice sounding through the door, a deep baritone that calls to me but I can't stop now. If I stop, I wont restart.

"Wren!"

I continue still.

"Wren!" this time my name is accompanied by a loud thud, the door to the bathroom rattling as something heavy is rammed into it.

I continue.

"Wren, I swear to fucking god! Open this fucking door!"

I don't.

I finish this line and move onto the next just as the door to the bathroom slams open, the wood finally

134

succumbing to the wrath of Alexander Silver.

He stands in the threshold, sweaty, out of breath and fucking angry.

And I make that push with the blade, slicing through my flesh to rid myself of the brand.

17

Lex

I head into the bedroom, feeling exhausted after the lack of sleep the night before. I expect to find Wren in the bed, still sleeping. Doc had said she would sleep a lot, to recover from all the shit she went through with Valentine but when I enter, I don't find her in the bed.

The sheets are rumbled, a breeze blowing in through the open window, the curtains swishing as it does. There are small splotches of blood on the white cotton and my eyes frantically search the room for her until they land on the dustbin outside the bathroom, filled with the used bandages from her wounds and the bathroom door closed.

I cross the room and press on the handle, finding it locked.

Her breathing is heavy from the other side, so loud I can hear every intake and exhale of breath. Can hear how it's filled with pain, a rattle of air that pushes forcefully from her lips.

"Wren!"

She doesn't respond.

"WREN!"

My shoulder slams into the door.

She doesn't respond to either my voice or my need to get in.

"Wren, I swear to fucking God. Open this fucking door!"

I get no response and I flip, a rage with no off button. I slam my shoulder into the door, once, twice, three times before the wood splinters and the lock comes away. The door slams into the wall on the other side, cracked down the middle and dangling from its hinges.

"What the fuck are you doing!?" I boom, unable to completely understand the picture before me.

Wren, naked, wet, bleeding, the blade from my razor grasped between her fingers as she runs the long edge down her thigh, peeling the skin away over the top of that fucking brand Valentine gave her. Her fingers ribboned with blood, sweat on her brow, dripping down her spine.

She meets my eyes, but I don't see anything there, just a soulless, dead and broken stare. Her eyes are bloodshot and her face twists with pain as she continues to mutilate herself.

Fuck.

"STOP!" I boom.

It's as if she cannot hear me.

I have no choice, I cross the space between us and rip the blade from her hand, feeling her blood mingle with mine as the same blade cuts into the palm of my hand.

"Get off me!" She screams, her fists pounding into my shoulders.

"What the fuck do you think you're doing!?"

"I'll fucking kill him!"

She thrashes and convulses as I grab her, hauling her over my shoulder as I take her back into the room, throwing her naked onto the bed. Her eyes are wild, my little bird isn't there at the moment, instead, she's being drowned by whatever this is.

She tries to get up, but I force her back down and as I hold her there, I reach across and open the top drawer of the cabinet by the bed. Her blood stains the sheets, runs over my skin and seeps through my clothes. Her eyes are wide, face twisted in anger, in pain and in sorrow. Tears leak from her eyes, sliding over her temples and into her hairline.

The nightmares might manifest themselves, the doc said, *it's unusual but not unseen in cases like this. If she doesn't calm, sedate her, it'll be like a reset for her mind.*

I've done a lot of bad shit in my time, but this feels wrong. Whilst I may not understand all this shit going on inside of my body, I know don't want to do this to her though I see no other way.

Again, she tries to get up, but I stop her, throwing her back down on the bed and using my weight to keep her there.

"I want to kill him!" She sobs, "But I need this gone, Lex, please. Take this brand off me!"

Her cries twist like a knife to the stomach.

"Please!"

"I'm sorry, baby. Forgive me."

I plunge the needle into her arm, compressing the plunger so all the medicine is deposited into her bloodstream. Her eyes widen, a look of shock and betrayal crossing her features before the sedative quickly takes hold and her arms drop, thudding against the mattress.

I see more tears pool in the corners of her eyes as she realizes what I have just done and then her lids shutter closed, and her body goes slack. Those tears continue to slip from her eyes, haunting me.

"FUCK!" I roar, climbing away from her and launching the needle across the room. "FUCK!"

There's a sudden whirl of activity as Ryker and several men storm into the room and I snap. A different type of fury fills me, this is primal, this is an explosion of protective rage that does not discriminate. Everything and everyone is a target.

"Get the fuck out!" I withdraw the gun from my side and level it at the nearest guy, I don't know his name, I don't care as I pull the trigger and shoot him. I move to the next guy but a quick hand lowering my arm abruptly stops me from shooting him too. The other men leave quickly, dragging the injured guy from the room as they depart, fleeing, until its only me, Ryker and Wren left here. I didn't kill him at least, a flesh wound at most.

My chest heaves with each inhale of breath, my eyes wide and teeth bared.

He doesn't once turn to look at her. He keeps his eyes solely trained on me. "Fix your woman, Lex."

My nostrils flare as anger and confusion and pure blinding rage run through my system like a rampaging bull. I watch him leave, his shoulders tense, spine ramrod straight and the click of the door closing is as loud as the gun I just fired.

Ryker's comment wasn't one to shame Wren, it was one of understanding. He knows what's happening to her and to me, something that would never happen to me. I have a weakness, one I've had for months now and I also know he'll be there to protect her with his life as much as I will be.

She lays sprawled on the bed, medicated and asleep, naked body with all the cuts, the bruises and scars Valentine subjected her to on show to me.

140

I see the canular discarded on the floor where she ripped it from her hand and also the new wound on her thigh where she tried to rid herself of the brand and realize this is way beyond my capabilities. Sighing, I pull my phone from my pocket and text Ryker, instructing him to get the doc here as soon as possible and in the meantime, I dress her, careful to avoid the wounds on her body.

A short time later, Wren now covered in a pair of my boxer shorts and a large undershirt, the doc arrives. He surveys her where she lays in the bed, the wound badly dressed by my hand but at least I've stemmed the bleeding.

"What happened?" The doc asks.

"Fix it."

He sighs and gets to work, first on the leg she mutilated. He unwraps the gauze I put on to stem the bleeding and sucks in a breath. "What happened?"

I shake my head, refusing to bring the images back to my head, "She tried to rid herself of the brand."

"This poor girl."

My brows pull down as the doc brings all the supplies he needs from the case. "She didn't deserve this."

He starts to clean it up, putting antiseptic fluid and other ointments onto the wound, wiping gently over the top and around the edges, "She could need a skin graft here." He says.

141

"Do what you must."

The doc sighs, "Do you think maybe she would be better off without you?"

This is the type of comment that would usually switch me in a matter of seconds but his words hit some deep rooted part of me that knows he is right. This, *this whole entire thing,* is my fault.

"Yeah, doc, I know."

He gets to work, and I leave him to it, positioning myself in the chair across from the bed, not interrupting him as he fixes up my little bird. When she's wrapped and medicated, he nods his head once and exits, leaving me with my sleeping woman.

There's a pile of medication on the cabinet next to me that I know I'll have to force her to take but right now I can watch her as she sleeps, as medically induced as it is.

At least like this she slightly resembles the woman I lost in the club all those weeks ago.

Her hair, now dry and wild like I remembered fans around her head like a fiery halo, her dark lashes resting on top of her cheeks as she dreams, hopefully something more pleasant than whatever is plaguing her every other time. The sedation will wear off soon but I can appreciate this time now.

She'll hate me when she wakes.

I knew whatever animosity she felt towards me was long gone, I knew I had her but how much damage is this going to do to the already precarious balance we had. Regardless of whether she wanted nothing to do with me, regardless of if she kicked and screamed and fought me, she was mine. I had her. I was never letting her go. I would not lose her again.

At my side is where she belonged. At my side is where she will stay.

18.

I wake to a grumble, a distressed sound, a mixture between sorrow and pain and when I open my eyes the room is in absolute darkness.

"Wren?" I ask.

"Stay the fuck away from me." Her voice is weak and yet her words hold a punch so hard I feel it in my gut. When had I become so weak that a woman could do this to me? I didn't hate it. Not when it was her.

She loved me, I knew she did and despite my belief that I was incapable of feeling the same, I loved her too.

She was mine. Irrevocably mine. There was no escape, no mercy, there was no way I was ever going to let my little bird go.

"That isn't how this works, little bird." I stand from my chair, stretching out the muscles that have been sat in the same position for too long.

"You drugged me!" I hear her climb from the bed, feel the anger radiating from her in waves that meet my own. Rage because she hurt herself. Rage because Valentine hurt her. Rage because this was a war I was losing.

"I did what I had to."

"You have no right!" She screams. I see her silhouette standing at the side of the bed, bathed in the moonlight streaming in through the window and I stand to match her stance.

"I have every right little bird or have you forgotten you belong to me now."

"I belong to no one."

"Do not test me now, little bird."

"Or what, Lex? You'll drug me again!?"

I storm her, finding her body in the darkness as if it is a beacon for my eyes and body. Her sharp intake of breath makes my heart rate spike and so quickly, in a way I know will not do her harm I have her pinned to the wall, her face cupped in my hand. My fingers sink into her flesh, holding her still, tilting her face towards mine as I press my nose against hers with my teeth bared.

"You think you can hurt yourself and get away with it?" I growl, "You think I'm going to sit here and watch you mutilate this body, this body that is *mine!*" My anger courses through me and I slam my free hand against the wall, the thump loud to my ears, "What you do with it is on my authority, how it is treated, worshipped, loved and pleasured is my responsibility."

"Fuck you!"

"You want me to fuck you, little bird, help you remember how it feels to be owned?" My cock twitches and I grind my hips forward, pressing into that sweet, sweet place between her legs. I hold her tightly, no space between us as I push her harder against the wall.

Her breathing becomes erratic, her heartrate pumping so wildly I feel it against my own chest.

"You want that? Did you miss me?" My lips brush across hers, barely a taste and yet fire erupts deep within my soul, "Have you missed my cock, baby? Let me help you remember how it feels for my dick to slide so deep into your fucking pussy that you forget your own name and the only thing you remember is me, the only name you scream, will be mine."

"Lex," her voice is a broken whisper, a mix between a cry and a moan.

"Let me help you forget," my tongue runs down the side of her face, the taste of her salty tears coating my tongue, "let me help you forget, *everything*."

"Yes."

I need no more convincing. I need her as badly as she needs me. I rip her from her clothes, shedding the material until I feel her body under my hands, the soft skin, the dips and curves. I have to be careful not to hurt her, but I can't stop myself. I unfasten my pants,

grabbing my cock when it is free to pump my hand up
the shaft, rubbing the bead of precum over the crown
before smearing it across her lower abdomen. Fuck, I
need her heat. I want her pussy convulsing on my dick. I
want her to forget it all, Valentine, the club, the pain and
torture, I want the only thing she remembers is me, my
name, my body, my cock. I grab her, pushing her up the
wall until her legs wrap around my hips and her arms
loop around my neck. My mouth sucks at her breasts, the
wild beat of her heart pulsing against my tongue and I
line up to her entrance, sliding in home and finding it
wet, welcoming and ready for me.

"I see you did miss me, little bird," I rasp against her
throat, pulsing my hips, "I missed you too. I've been
crazy without you."

"Lex," she cries, rolling her hips so her clit rubs against
me, smearing her arousal over my skin the same way I
did hers. My fingers knead her ass, the flesh pliant
beneath my grip as I pound into her, her walls clamping
and convulsing on my cock.

"Tell me little bird or have you forgotten."

When she doesn't answer I pull us both away from the
wall, spinning and dropping us both to the bed, settling
myself in the cradle of her thighs, knees to the edge of
the mattress.

"Say it!" I growl.

I let one leg – the inured one – drop to the mattress and
then force the other up further, holding it at the back of
the thigh, opening her up further for me to slam my hips

forward. Our hips clash as I penetrate deep.

Wren screams, her back arching from the bed.

"Little bird," I coo, "Tell me."

"You," she cries, "I'm yours!"

"Good girl," I drop down to my elbows, nuzzling my nose into her hair as I roll my hips slowly but no less deep, "Such a good girl."

Her nails score my back, drawing blood as I lose myself in her. I'd been without her for too long and I vow, here and now, as my balls tighten and her walls clamp down around me, her orgasm drawing my own from my body, that she'll never leave my side again. I empty myself in her, my teeth biting her flesh, her scream echoing from the walls and then we lay there, in the darkness, in silence.

"I need it gone," she whispers, "This doesn't change anything, Alexander, I want this mark off me, and if you do not help me, I'll do it myself."

My hand strokes up the centre of her chest, through the valley of her breast until my hand caresses her delicate throat, "Do not make threats, little bird, I will help you, but you must first heal."

She swallows against my palm, "I'll kill him." She declares.

"I hope you do little bird, I want to see you bathed in his blood."

She curls into me, wincing a little in pain so I get up and move to the cabinet, grabbing the painkillers and antibiotics the doc left. Surprisingly she takes them with ease and curls up at my side, resting her head on the soft spot between my neck and shoulder. Her breath fans across my chest, her hair draped over my arm whilst her finger lazily draws circles on my stomach. She sleeps and for the first time in weeks, I do too.

I would complain that the morning is here too quickly however I find no such thing when I wake to Wren kissing her way down my stomach, over the ridges of my abdominal muscles, all the way down until her mouth hovers over my cock.

A grin curves up my lips as her eyes flick to me, a life there I didn't see in her before. Here she looks wild, free, a little mischievous as her tongue slips from between her lips and she licks me from the base all the way to the tip.

When she wraps her mouth around my dick, my hips surge from the bed, seeking the heat of her tongue as she sucks, swallowing me down until I hit the back of her throat. I wondered how long I'd get to keep this version of Wren before the nightmares begin again, how long her mind will remain here rather than in the past, remembering all the things Valentine did to her. I don't think she'll truly be free of her horrors until we see Valentine dead and it's something I'll give her. My gift to the queen of the city. Slowly she draws away from me, dropping to her knees at the edge of the bed and I stand, staring down at her as her small palm wraps around my cock and she retakes me into her mouth.

"That's it, little bird," I praise, slowly pumping my hips

to match her pace, tangling my hand into her hair and wrapping the copper strands around my fingers, "such a good girl, on your knees for me."

She hums on my cock, forcing herself down further, enough to make her gag reflex kick in but I don't give her a reprieve, I fist the hair the back of her head tightly, forcing her back down, reveling in the feel of her on my cock. I'll have her every way. Her nails dig into my thighs as I begin to fuck her mouth, her eyes watering, tongue lapping and licking.

"You're going to fucking swallow it," I tell her, teeth gritted and voice nothing more than a primal growl, my orgasm impending and she gives the barest of nods. My grunt, a moan of pleasure as her other hand slides up the inside of her thigh to cup my balls echoes through the room, her hand squeezing almost to the point of pain, and I can't control it. My orgasm whips through me and I spill into her mouth with a roar, coating her tongue, her throat as my cock pulses wildly, my balls emptying themselves into her willing mouth. I withdraw myself and she smirks up at me, one brow raised as she gently wipes her lips with the tips of her fingers.

"On your fucking back," I order.

Never taking her eyes from mine, she lowers herself gently until she's laid completely bare on the carpet.

"Touch yourself."

Her hand slips down her stomach, fingers falling between her thighs as she spreads her pussy and gently caresses her clit, swollen and ready. Her arousal glistens, coating her fingers as she plays.

"Keep your eyes on me," I tell her when her lids threaten to close under the pleasure of what she is doing to herself.

She slips a finger inside, using the heel of her hand to apply friction at the same time, and rolls her hips, the sweet sound of her arousal loud in the otherwise quiet bedroom.

I'm already growing hard again watching her and so I wrap a hand around my cock, pumping it to the same speed she fucks herself with her finger.

"On your fucking knees!" I order, "Now!"

Slowly, she rolls before raising on her knees, spine arched so she's still able to toy with herself and leaving my cock, I drop behind her, pushing her hand away in favor of my tongue. She pushes her ass back, wanting more of my mouth on her pussy so I spread her and punch my tongue into her entrance before licking and sucking at her flesh.

Before she can climax, I pull away, rising up onto my knees and reveling in the view before me, even bruised and a little broken, she's a fucking angel for the devil to feast his eyes upon. Her ass, on show for my eyes, spine curved, body heaving with each labored breath. I run a finger down her ass, through her cheeks, finding her virgin flesh, teasing with the tip of my finger.

She sucks in a breath as I tease it forward, finding resistance. "Lex," she moans.

"It's coming."

I smear some of her arousal up through her cheeks and then line myself up with her entrance, slamming forward as my finger teases and slips in, making her spine arch further, her ass pushing back.

"Yes!" She screams.

I fuck her like this, her body meeting mine thrust for thrust, slamming and biting and screaming, her cries of ecstasy bouncing off the walls and meeting me, spurring me on to go harder, faster. Skin slaps together, bodies grinding, finding a high I'll never be able to find unless I'm buried inside of her body, hearing her moans, tasting her pleasure.

I hold her hip with my spare hand, my other still at her ass, fucking her virgin flesh with my finger whilst my cock pounds into her body relentlessly. The carpet burns against my knees, my fingers tightening as she draws out the pleasure.

"Oh, God," she cries, "fuck."

"Not God, little bird," I pull from her ass and lean forward, licking my way up her spine, tasting the salt on her skin, as I continue to roll my hips, pushing into her hard but slow, "But your very own fucking devil."

"Lex," She cries, "Please!"

"For you, little bird, anything," I straighten, tuck one hand around her hips to pinch her clit roughly between my fingers and then fuck her hard and fast, slamming into her again and again. She screams my name over and over as we both tumble over that edge, disappearing into the abyss of our own making.

19.

I feel a wetness slipping down my thigh, a warm, thick liquid that tickles as it rolls over my skin.

"You're bleeding," Lex grumbles, pulling out abruptly. I wince at the loss of him, dropping down onto the carpet, the pain a sudden onset that grips me and has my body alighting in raging flames. It was too much too soon, but even so, even with my nerves lit up like a live wire, I can't find it in me to regret it. Not when Lex consumed me so thoroughly, not when the feel of him pressed against my body, buried so deep inside chased away the darkness and shadows that continued to plague me. When Lex comes back into the room he's dressed in sweats, bare chested, and surprise, he doesn't look happy.

His eyes narrow in on the blood streaming down my thigh but if he thinks I'm going to apologize for what I did, he can forget it. They're all thinking I'm weak, broken, unable to understand what I'm doing but I haven't seen anything as clear as I do now.

Alexander Silver was both my monster and my savior, but he wasn't the villain in my story. Not yet at least, the villain, the evil, the darkness in my story was my own father. I knew this. Did I go about it the right way? No, but I don't regret it. He doesn't get to win. He doesn't get to *own* me in this way. I don't belong to him. *I belong to me*. Lex likes to believe I belong to him and whilst he has my heart and my body, I am still me.

I will always be me.

Without saying a word, Lex kneels on the floor next to me, unwrapping the bandage from my leg, slowly, as if afraid of what he is going to see on the other side. I wasn't afraid. It was a start of getting my revenge.

He did this to me but it won't break me.

But I'll break him.

He's underestimated me.

And that was his second mistake. The first being crossing Alexander in the first place.

My thigh is a mess. The skin raw, open and weeping clear liquid along with the blood, oozing from my flesh like a leaky tap.

"You ever do something like this again," Lex growls, his teeth grinding, the threat left hanging in the air between us.

I roll my eyes, gritting my teeth as he starts to clean up the wound with alcohol. The breath hisses through my teeth as he swipes across the open wound, cleaning away the blood.

"I'm serious Wren," He pins me with a look so icy, my heart stutters.

"I understand."

His eyes narrow but ultimately, he says nothing and continues to clean me up before wrapping the wound in a new gauze and shoving painkillers and antibiotics into my hand.

"Come downstairs," he orders, "Eat with me."

I nod and watch him leave, dragging my naked ass from the floor in search of clothes and brushing my teeth. When I'm dressed in loose fitting pants and a sweater, my hair tied in a knot atop my head, I take the stairs and step into the hall, greeted by a mass of huge bodies, guns strapped to their hips, poised, ready, lethal. They each nod their head at me as I pass them, watching in a way that feels protective, like they're ready to leap in front of a bullet for me. It freaks me the fuck out.

When I turn into the kitchen, I don't find Lex but I do find Ryker.

"Gruff!"

His eyes widen before settling back down, a small tilt of his lips giving away his pleasure at seeing me. I knew he liked me. The burly fucker.

"Wren," he nods.

"Oh, don't be so serious, Gruff, we're alive."

"Barely," he grumbles.

"Oh, shh," I pout, heading for the coffee machine, "Where's Lex?"

"Dealing with shit."

I cock a brow, "Care to elaborate?"

"Not particularly."

I make my coffee and sit opposite him, cocking my head as I take in the tiredness in his face, the dark shadows beneath his eyes and the downward turn of his mouth. I mean the guy had a face of stone but this was more.

"What's going on with you?"

"Has your friend always been this difficult?" He blurts.

"My friend?"

"Aurora."

The blood drains from my face, my heart rate plummeting and I have to grip the table to stop myself from falling from the chair.

"Where is she?"

"I'll take this," Lex's deep baritone fills the room like a blast from a speaker.

Gruff's eyes dart from me to Lex before he nods once, plucks his coffee from the table and exits.

"Where is she, Alexander?"

I stand, still using the table for support.

My best friend was here, under the same roof.

"Safe."

"*Where!?*"

"Come, little bird," he beckons me with a curl of his finger, and blindly I follow, crossing the space and watching his body before me, slowly take the stairs and turn at the end of the hall. I forgot how damn big this place was and it feels like several minutes pass before we stop at a door.

"Is she in there?"

"Yes."
"Let me in."

"Wren, she isn't the same girl you remember."

"Alexander. Let me in."

He closes his eyes and unlocks the door, pushing it open and stands back, allowing me room to enter.

The room is darkened by the curtains drawn though not so dark I can't see inside. A bed, some drawers and a couple of doors leading to an en suite and walk in wardrobe. There's a shape on the bed, a curved womanly shape that lifts the white sheets from the mattress, moving steadily with a person breathing deeply.

"Rory?"

The person on the bed goes completely still, any and all movement ceases to the point I worry they have stopped breathing but then a voice cracks the silence, so small, fragile, cracked and hoarse, "Wren?"

"Yeah, Rory, it's me."

"Where have you been?"

I stop at the end of the bed, feeling Alexander's presence behind me but not too close, allowing me some space to speak with my friend.

"I've been sick." I wouldn't tell her exactly, but I'm sure she knew it wasn't an illness.

"Me too," she sighs heavily.

"Are you okay?"

A long silence draws between us, and what I thought would be a happy reunion between two best friends is turning worse with every second that passes between us.

"I don't know." She answers.

"Can I help?"

"I think you put me in this mess, Wren, I was doing

okay, ya know?"

The words shatter my heart, "I'm sorry, Rory, I didn't mean for this to happen."

"But it happened, and that's, I'll survive."

"Rory…"

"They raped me, Wren. *Raped* me. Countless times. Over and over. I was choked. Beaten. They chained me up and spread me open so one, two, three men could come in and do whatever the fuck they wanted and then I find out that the man who had me kidnapped in the first place is *your father*. He watched. He watched it happen. And every time he watched he spoke about how this was going to happen to you. How all of this was going to happen to you, and I couldn't bear it Wren. I didn't want this to happen to you, so I tried to tell them we didn't know each other. That we weren't that close but then you went and did that stupid fucking thing and gave yourself up. To what? Protect me? Why!?"

"I'll always protect you, Rory."

"What did they do to you?"

I suck in a ragged breath, "Enough."

"Wren, I'm sorry. If it wasn't for me, maybe you wouldn't be here either."

"Don't!" I growl. "Don't you fucking dare!" My voice goes up a pitch as emotion clings to my every being, threatening to overtake me but I will not allow Marcus

Valentine to have any more of me, even if he is not here to see it. "None of this is on you. I will protect you no matter the cost, there is nothing you can do about it."

Lex's hand wraps around my shoulder, a calming presence to settle the rising storm within me. It works, I fear it'll always work. I scoff inwardly, how things have changed. I met a monster only a few weeks ago and yet it is the same monster that settles the demons brewing inside of me.

His breath strokes my neck, warm and scented with smoke and whiskey but not unpleasant, "Easy now, little bird."

"Is this him?" Rory asks.

"Yes."

"This is your fault," she hisses.

Lex stiffens behind me but stays quiet. I know it's for me, but I can't help but feel defensive over him. He is my demon. My devil. His sins are my own. When I whisper to the darkness, it's his voice that answers.

"Rory, there is a lot you do not understand."

"Please leave." She suddenly requests, "I don't want to talk anymore."

"Rory..."

"Please," her voice cracks, "now I know you're alive and okay, I can sleep."

"Okay," my own emotion clogs my throat, making it rough and raspy, "you sleep, Rory. We'll talk tomorrow."

She doesn't answer me so Lex steers me from the room, guiding me out the door and then closes it softly behind him before locking it.

"You're keeping her prisoner?" I hiss under my breath.

"No little bird, she is a danger to everyone and herself, she needs to be kept here until we can be sure she is safe."

"Why?"

"Because she means something to you, Wren, and what you care for will always be important."

I fall into his chest, trying to stop the tears from falling but failing. I don't want to cry. I don't want to feel anything but this much emotion is too much to stifle. Marcus Valentine doesn't deserve this and yet I do it anyway, crying into Lex's chest like he's my lifeline, the only thing keeping me afloat in turbulent waters.

His hand smooths down my hair, his other arm holding me as close to his body as physically possible.

"Shh now, little bird, you will have your vengeance."

I picture it, I taste it on my tongue. Valentine, *my father,* bleeding out before me, not from a gun shot or an easy wound but a wound that would cause a slow, painful death, I taste the copper tang of blood on my tongue and feel it running over my skin. It's the only thing that stops the tears. Knowing that his days are numbered and it is only a matter of time before I have him before me.

"Promise me." I say suddenly.

"What little bird?"

"That when the time comes, I get to kill him."

"Wren…"

"Lex, I need to do it. For me. For you. For your mother." I stare up into his silver eyes, seeing the confliction there, the need to protect, "he took so much from me, so much from you and I want to do it for you and *me.*"

"We will see."

I don't push him, as much as I want to, this is something that will need to be discussed. I laugh at myself, had I thought this would become of my life only a mere few weeks ago? Planning a murder? Planning vengeance for both me and a man I deemed a devil but became so much more than that between then and now?

He presses the most tender of kisses to my forehead and then steers me towards the stairs, "Let's eat."

I agree and follow him down the stairs, watching all his glory move and ripple, the muscle and the sinew, an unleashed fury buried not so far from the surface.

And he was mine.

20

I watch her from across the table, those dainty hands, her small and yet undefeatable body, the way her eyes have seemed take on a steel coating as if the world could come at her but she would stand atop it all and break everyone who dare try to defeat her.

It's a far cry from the girl Kingston delivered to my arms. A far cry from the girl I thought I would never get back.

All it does is make me harder than a fucking rock inside my pants.

My little bird is not so little anymore. She's a fucking phoenix, rising from the ashes to destroy our enemies. She's a goddess, a formidable presence that when crossed will simply explode to protect what she loves the most.

She wraps her perfect lips around the fork to slide the piece of meat from the tongs into her mouth and flicks her eyes to me, quirking one brow as if to ask me what is going on inside my head.

We needed to discuss things. Things separate to the shit burning our kingdom to the ground around us. Things that simply cannot be ignored.

Did I deserve her dying words?

Of course not.

Was I going to ignore them? That's a big fucking no.

"Little bird," I coo, finishing my dinner and placing my cutlery on the plate before me.

"Twisted king," she smirks.

I laugh, leaning back in my chair as I watch her across the table.

She finishes her plate and then leans back in her chair, cocking her eyebrow, "Something the matter?"

"We need to discuss things."

"What is there to talk about?"

"Back at the club," flashbacks of the fire raging around us, the blood spilling from her body, staining the ground beneath where she lay freezes my tongue. My eyes squeeze shut. Her, right there, a wound that should have been fatal spurting blood from her abdomen, rivers of crimson running over her pale skin, her breath slow and shallow. Her dying and me not being able to save her. Her being ripped from me.

A body before me brings me back to the now and when I open my eyes I see her there, fiery hair, emerald green eyes, holding a fire that only belonged in hell within them but dulled, soft, warm as she stares up at me. "Tell me."

"You said you loved me. Was that true?"
I couldn't help but feel like a little boy at this point. But I had to ask. I needed to know.

She sits back onto her heels and cocks her head, a small, devious smile curving her lips, "Why, Lex, are we feeling a little insecure?"

"Little bird, do not push me."

Her smile only curves higher on her mouth but she does not toy, she leans forward, pressing her delectable mouth to mine, "Yes it was true."

"You love me?"

She sits back but far from relaxed. "Yes. Lex, I love you, though I'm sure it'll leave me as damned as you are."

A grin carves my lips.

"Don't be so smug."

"How can I not?"

"Because I doubt this is a victory."

"It is a victory, my little bird," I drag her to my lap, positioning her in a way that means she has to straddle my lap and feel how much her words affect me, "for I have won the most prized possession of all."

"What's that?" she breathes, mouth hovering above mine.

"You."

I waste no more seconds, I slam my mouth onto hers, pushing my tongue between her lips, tasting her, claiming her once more. She was mine as much as I was hers.

"I am in love with you too," I admit, "I never thought it possible, but I love you, little bird. All and every part of you."

"Alexander," she breaths, rolling her hips.

My cock grows ever harder.

Shit. The things she does to me should be forbidden.

"And so the monster can love, after all," she presses her mouth to mine, tentative, soft and unsure.

"Who thought it possible," I chuckle, letting my hands roam down her curves to cup her waist. When my hand brushes her wound, she winces, body tensing on mine.

"Are you finished?" I ask.

She nods so I guide her from my lap and towards the stairs, up to the master bedroom and then the bathroom where I begin to draw a bath. I pop a couple of pills from the packet the doc left including the antibiotics and cross to where Wren sits on the bed. She takes them without argument, following them down with some water before I guide her to the bath, helping her strip from her clothes.

The marks on her body cause my heart to speed, a rage so hot and blinding rushing my system. I don't know if I'll be able to give her what she wishes for with Valentine. I have no idea if I'll be able to stop myself when the time comes.

She climbs into the steaming water, eyes squeezed closed as the water washes over the wounds on her body but once the sting settles she relaxes, leaning back and submerging herself more. I sit on the edge of the bath, just watching her, witnessing the stress lines on her face ease, her brow relaxing and her mouth flattening as she fully settles. Her copper hair floats on the surface of the water, and the steady rhythm of her breathing gently ripples the water.

Unable to stop myself, I lean forward, following the curve of her jaw with the tip of my finger. She leans into the touch, lashes fluttering as I move down her throat to her collar bones, her smooth skin so warm beneath the pad of my finger.

"Come in here with me," she whispers.

She keeps her eyes closed as I strip from my clothes and only when I'm ready, she sits up so I can slide in behind her. She leans back against my chest, rolling her head to the side to look up at me.

"Have you heard from Kingston?" she asks.

My nostrils flare, "Whilst we are naked together, little bird, please refrain from muttering another mans name."

She smirks, "That's not the answer I was looking for."

"I see you still cannot hold your tongue." I kiss her forehead, "he'll be arriving in the next few days."

"Do you know what he wants?"

"No, but let's not think about that right now," I push her wild hair away from her face, "let me love you, little bird."

Her eyes go soft as I lean down to kiss her perfectly delectable mouth. I was never going to get enough of this woman.

.

· 21 ·

I lay in the dark, staring up at the ceiling. A gentle breeze teases the curtains at the window and Lex's soft breathing is a comfort at my side and yet I cannot sleep. Every time I close my eyes I see him, the deranged look in his eyes, the malice and evil rooted so deep the only way to cure it is to put him down.

No one knows where he is. His men have scattered, his usual hide outs left deserted like no one was ever there. How does a man disappear like that?

Part of me wonders if he's already been taken out and whilst that should bring me a little comfort, it just twists my gut. I still hear the screams of the girls he had down in that prison, the cries and whimpers, the grunts and groans, I fear they'll haunt me forever. I know the girls are now safe but forever changed.

My mind wanders back to Rory, locked away in a room in this very house.

She may be free of Valentine and the sick fucks he has employed but she's not the same girl.

But then neither was I.

Slowly, I push back the covers and slip soundlessly from the bed, careful not to disturb Alexander. He stirs momentarily and I hold my breath, waiting to see if he'll wake but when he doesn't, I grab one of his shirts and slip it on before creeping to the door and opening it, wincing when it creaks in the otherwise silent house. Looking over my shoulder, Lex still hasn't woken so I slip into the darkened hallway and wait.

I'm not stupid enough to believe we were alone in this house but there was no one immediately in the area so I continue until I'm outside of Rory's bedroom.

The lock on the door is open which causes me to pause, but instead of questioning it, I push on the handle and go inside.

There's a light on, its dim ambience casting a dull orange glow throughout the room. The large bed is centered on the far wall, close to a window and when I look over, it isn't just one shape I see in the bed, but two.

Rory's pale blonde air is fanned out on the pillow behind her, and she is curled on her side, pressing into a much larger body which holds her protectively. I recognize Gruff immediately, his shaggy hair a mess on his head, his thick arms banded around her, so big they make her look more pixie like than anything else and they look...*peaceful.*

What the actual fuck?

"Sneaking away in the middle of the night," Alexander

whispers behind me, making me jump. One hand comes down onto my arm to steady me whilst the other covers my mouth to stop the scream as he gently coaxes me back out the door. "Anyone might think you want to run away from me still, little bird."

He takes his hand away, "No, I just," I frown, looking back at the door which Lex is pulling closed, "What the hell is that?"

Lex pinches the bridge of his nose, "Ryker is helping her."

"By fucking her!?" I hiss under my breath, "fuck, Lex, do you know what she went through!?"

Anger courses through my veins, I wanted to go back in there and rip Gruff out of that bed if only to protect my best friend.

"They're not fucking," Lex growls, "Now, back to bed."

I huff but let him push me back towards the bedroom, confused as all hell. "I don't understand."

"Nightmares."

"Huh?"

"She's suffering with night terrors, Ryker appears to keep them away."

I puff my cheeks, filling them with air and then blow it out harshly, still not grasping this whole thing. Ryker. Lex's second hand, a man almost as ruthless as Lex, giving comfort to a broken girl…

"Don't think too much about it."

Lex shuts the door and pushes me towards the bed, "Why aren't you sleeping?" he asks.

"I couldn't"

The back of my knees hit the bed and I sit, staring up at him as he advances, body shrouded in shadow and only a slight glow lighting up the harsh edges of his face. He looks both terrifying and delicious all the same.

"Have I ever told you how much I like you in my shirts?" He muses, leaning forward to pluck the top button open, "but not as much as I like it off."

I don't stop him as he flicks all the buttons on the shirt open and I still don't as he pushes the material to the side and gently pushes me back so I'm led flat on the bed with my legs dangling over the sides.

I don't see his eyes taking in every inch of me, but I feel them as they caress me, as thorough as his hands, looking at all of me like I'm a piece of art hanging on a wall. I may have felt that way before but I'm scarred now, wounds and bruises littering my skin.

As if sensing where my thoughts have just gone to, Lex snaps, "Don't you fucking dare."

I swallow.

He drops to his knees so suddenly I don't have time to

keep up with his movements and then his mouth is on my stomach, pressing kisses over the almost healed wound in my stomach, right on top of the raised and angry pink skin. He moves over my stomach and chest, kissing each bruise and cut before he moves to my neck, my shoulders, arms and then he's at my legs, pressing butterfly kisses to the inside of the thigh where Valentine branded me.

Arousal heats the space between my legs and my stomach knots, pushing those thoughts from my mind as his mouth drags across my thigh, kissing all the areas where I'm now marked. He doesn't give a fuck.

When his mouth lands on my pussy I gasp, the sound loud in the quiet room. His tongue swipes from bottom to top, the flat edge of his tongue dragging through my folds before stopping at my clit and sucking it into his mouth, the sound obscene and dirty and yet oh so right.

My hands fly to his head, fingers gripping his hair to hold him in place as he flicks his tongue, sending me higher and higher.

The king is on his knees for me.

"Shit," I hiss.

His fingers suddenly thrust inside of me, curling and already finding that one sweet spot inside me, rubbing it expertly until my thighs are shaking and I'm gasping for air, begging for both mercy and more.

I'm right there when he suddenly pulls away.

"Do you want more?" He asks.

"Yes," I beg, "Please."

"Who do you belong to, little bird?"

"You. Always you. Only you."

"You're such a good girl."

 He slides his boxers from his hips and down his legs before dropping down once more to kiss me between the legs and then he's lining himself up to my pussy, sinking in torturously slow.

 My eyes roll back in my head as he fills me and continues to do so at a pace that will kill me if he doesn't do something.

 When he's fully sheathed, he drops down to his elbows, holding himself there as he rests his forehead against my own. He begins to pump his hips, sliding out before slamming back in still too slow for my liking.

 "Fuck me," I growl, "I want you to *fuck me*."

 His mouth slams down onto mine, his tongue forcing entry as he continues that slow, torturous pace.

 When he pulls away, a wicked grin tugs at his mouth, "say please."

 "Please."

 "Anything for you," he chuckles darkly.

Pushing up, he stands at the edge of the bed, dragging me further down the bed and forcing my ass up before he slams into me so hard my bones rattle.

"Like this, baby?"

"Yes!"

He slams his hips into me, our skin slapping together, the sound echoing in this quiet space. Perspiration wets my skin and my whole body coils tight, ready to snap at any moment.

"I want it," Lex growls, "I want to feel you come on my cock, now, little bird."

"Lex," I rasp.

He fucks me like I'm his lifeline, like I'm the air that fills his lungs and the blood that pumps through his veins and he continues until he's drawing out a climax so shattering I'll never be put together again. Stars burst behind my eyes and all my muscles cramp and then release, my pussy contracting wildly, ripping a scream from my throat so loud I'm sure the whole house hears it.

"Fuck!" He roars, fucking me harder, more relentlessly before he slams home once more, and then stills, his climax filling me, his cock jerking with his release.

For a few minutes we lay there in the dark, bodies stuck together, breathing hard and fast.

Lex fills the silence, "Don't you ever think you are

anything but perfection."

 I don't have a chance to respond when he pulls away from me and crosses the room, slamming the bathroom door which has been replaced since he rammed his way through it only a few days ago. I lay there in the dark, feeling him leak onto my thighs and wait for him to return.

22

This much rage has no output, no way to be released. There's only one thing I know that will remedy it and he is still yet to be found.

My hands grip the marble counter, my chest heaving with each breath I take, trying to steady the fury I feel sliding through my veins. I can still smell her on my skin, my cock is still wet with her arousal, the sweat beading on my skin and yet fucking her has not released a single ounce of this tension.

And I know why.

It's no longer a game to keep the city, no longer revenge for the murder of my mother but it's something else entirely. It is justice for my woman, it is ensuring she never has to see his face unless it's ripped away from his shoulders.

I splash cold water on my face once I've calmed a little more and then climb into the shower, allowing the heat to release some of the tension coiling my muscles. I hear the door open and Wren enter but I don't turn to her as she climbs into the shower behind me, wrapping her arms around my waist and leaning her cheek to my spine. Her breathing is a balm on my soul, her presence a beacon cutting a path through the darkness.

One hand is flat against my abdominal muscles, the other resting over my left pec, my heartbeat beneath her palm.

I take in a deep breath, dropping my head so the water hits me in the back of the skull.

We stay like that, her curled and plastered to my back whilst I calm, fingers gently whispering against my skin.

Wren eats her breakfast quietly, seemingly lost in her head as she takes small bites of the toast on the plate in front of her and gently sips her coffee. Dark shadows line her eyes from lack of sleep but overall, she appears to be getting healthier once more, the weight she lost in the time she was with Valentine slowly filling her back out and the glow under her skin becoming more vibrant every day. I'm sifting through emails when Ryker stumbles into the kitchen, still sleep mused and in the same clothes he wore yesterday.

Wren instantly shoots to her feet, crossing the space between them before she's jabbing her finger in his face, "I swear to god, if you touch a single finger on her body,

Ryker, I will kill you."

"Excuse me?" Ryker squares his shoulders, on high alert. He won't touch Wren but it raises my hackles nonetheless.

"Rory."

Ryker's head snaps back, offended, "What the fuck is your problem!?" He growls.

"Watch it." I snap.

"No," Ryker hisses, "why the fuck would you even fucking say shit like that? I'm not your fucking father, Wren."

I stand from the table abruptly, stepping up to Wren as she takes a step back, her hands clenching at her sides, "Enough!"

"Then why the fuck are you sleeping with her?" Wren growls.

"Because she's fucking scarred," Ryker furiously taps at his temple, "She's broken. Won't sleep. Won't eat, won't even fucking shower and for whatever *fucked* up reason, the only way I can get her to calm is if I fucking hold her!"

I had told Wren this though I couldn't blame her for not believing me, but she didn't know Ryker like I did. There were lines we wouldn't cross, even for us, the Silver family have never used or extorted women, let alone human beings for profit, it wasn't something that interested us. The skin trade was a seedy, dirty place to be and there were better ways to make money.

Valentine however wasn't just trading, he was in it. Allowing his men in on the business, letting those girls be beaten, tortured and raped before he sold them off like livestock, something that would have happened to Wren had Kingston not been the one to 'buy' her in return for protection.

The reminder turns the breakfast I ate sour. I fucking owed him.

I hated debt.

Fucking hated it.

It was worth Wren's life and I'll pay, even if I loathed the idea.

"I need to see her, maybe I'll be able to get through to her," Wren murmurs, leaning back on me further, Ryker's words sinking under her skin.

"I'm not sure that's a good idea, Wren," Ryker softens, reaching out to touch Wren's arm.

She stiffens but doesn't pull away and he drops his arm, flicking his eyes to me.

When was it that women became more important than anything else in this business?

Before, I would have done everything to see this city thrive, burn everything to the ground to ensure the Silver name stayed on top but now, I'd level the entire thing to the ground if it meant keeping my little bird safe.

Fuck.

"I've known her since we were teenagers, we've been through some shit, I can help."

With a sigh, Ryker shrugs and looks to me for approval. With a nod, I let Wren go, watching her as she quickly marches from the room and around the corner.

"Aurora isn't the same person."

"I know but Wren needs to understand that herself."

"There's nothing in the room she can hurt her with," Ryker huffs, dropping into the seat Wren vacated, "I've had word that Kingston has landed."

I pinch the bridge of my nose, "We need this shit sorted, the sooner the better. I have rats to kill."

"You not think it odd that Valentine is untraceable? Even when he was hiding, there was still a trace, now there is nothing. Not even his men have been spotted, it's like they never existed."

"The fucker is a coward, gone completely underground since he pissed off both us and the Hearts. If he knows what's good for him, he'll turn his gun on himself."

Ryker scoffs, "that won't happen."

"No," I sigh, "this city is going to shit."

"We'll get it back," Ryker taps his knuckles on the table, "best go make arrangements for the King of England."

My laughter is a quick huff of breath through my nostrils and a shake of my head.

I watch him leave and then I'm left with my thoughts, my mind whirling back to the safe house.

It would be wise to ship both Wren and Rory over there, give them twenty-four seven protection, security, weapons, and everything they could ever need to ride out this storm. I'd lose my fucking mind if something were to happen to Wren again and with Valentine still at large and the Syndicate breathing down my neck, I can't help but feel like it's inevitably going to happen, only this time round would she survive?

Beyond this shit, I have plans.

Plans for her and me, plans that involve continuing this line of Silver's, plans to have her with my ring on her finger, my surname gracing her name, and her swollen and pregnant with my child.

I want it all.

And for the first time I don't think I'm going to get it.

23

I don't knock as I turn the key and open the door.
Darkness greets me on the other side and a noise akin to
a child weeping, not a tantrum or a wail, but a soft,
sorrow filled cry, one that seeps into your skin and
buries itself into your soul. It's a cry of pain, pure,
unadulterated pain and with each sob and intake of
breath I feel that pain burrowing its way into my
marrow.

 "Aurora?" I whisper to the darkness.

With the curtains drawn all the way and all the lights off
I can barely see into the room, but I can just about make
out the outline of her body beneath the blankets on the
bed.

The sobs stop when she hears my voice and she rolls
onto her back, inhaling sharply.

 "Why are you here?"

 "I want to help, Rory, please let me help."

"There's nothing you can do, Wren."

"They hurt me too," I say to her, "and I would do it again, take it all again if it meant protecting you."

"But it didn't protect me, did it?" She snaps, sitting up abruptly, "Because before I even knew you were there, they had already done everything you'd never even dream of happening to you. They'd already taken *everything*. They ripped me apart."

"I'm sorry."

"Why?" She asks.

"Why am I sorry?"

"Yes, why are you sorry, Wren?"

"Because this never should have happened."

"Did you do it?" She asks. "Did you strap me down and hurt me Wren? Did you tell them to take me? Did you tell them to take turns?"

"No, Rory."

"Then why are you sorry, everyone keeps saying they're sorry. Sorry it happened. Sorry no one came sooner, but ultimately, what does an apology fix?"

I stay silent as she sits there in the middle of the bed, her body barely visible in the shadows of the bedroom but her breathing is heavy and filled with so much grief.

Ryker was right. She was broken and I didn't know how to help. I wanted to help. I wanted to fix it.

I would never be able to take it away but I wanted to get revenge, I wanted to get her through this.

"I came from nothing," she continues, "I had nothing, but I was starting to get something. I moved away from the only place I knew as home, to get away from the trouble I knew would follow me if I didn't. I was going to be a teacher, Wren. A teacher but how can I ever do any of that now?"

"You still can, Rory, this does not define you." I cross the room and pause before her, "can I sit?"

She sighs, "Sure."

"Ryker," I say, "He's helping you?"

She shrugs, "Some."

"What else can we do? Whatever it is, I'll do it, Rory."

She needed a therapist, a doctor, she needed help and I couldn't give her everything, but I would do as much as I possibly could.

She deserved the life she was fighting so damn hard for, she deserved everything she had worked to get and this, I needed to believe this was only going to be a set back, a huge one, one that will stay with her forever, but I knew she could be what she wanted to be.

I knew it. She just needed to believe it. It wasn't that

easy, I knew that, I was suffering with my own troubles that would no doubt stay with me forever, like this will her, but there has to be a way I can help her.

I climb onto the bed, shimmying my way towards her before I pull her into a huge hug, so fierce I hope she feels it right down to her soul.

"It's going to take time," I tell her, not letting go, "It'll take time, but I know, *I fucking know* you. I know you can do this. I know you hate me right now. I know this is my fault, I know I dragged you into this but I'm going to be here, I am going to help you and give you everything you need. Whatever it is you want, you need, you ask for, I'm going to give it to you."

"Wren," she cries, turning her face into my shoulder.

"I know, Rory. There's so much darkness in this world, but you already knew that, look where you came from and look at what you have achieved."

"I hate this feeling."

"What feeling?"

"It isn't even about what happened," Rory says, "I can deal with that. I can move on from that, over time, you know?" She pauses, "It's the idea, the fear, that it'll happen again."

"It won't happen again," I growl fiercely.

"You can't know that, and I'd rather be dead than do it again."

My heart stutters in my chest, an overwhelming panic settling into my skin, "Don't say that."

"I mean it."

Rory finally falls asleep, her head resting on my stomach as I smoothed her hair, and gently I move her from my body, positioning her head on the pillows before I climb off, leaving her curled on the bed. She appears to be sleeping soundly but I'll be back in the next thirty minutes to check on her again.

I will stay by her side every minute of every day if that's what it takes. My father will not take anything else from me.

I gently close the door but don't feel the need to lock it. She shouldn't be locked away, she needs freedom, normality, there is no need to take her from one cage and place her in another, no matter how gilded it is.

I take the stairs slowly, pressing my fingers into the centre of my forehead, trying to ease the tension I feel building there.

I'm not paying any attention when I hit the ground floor and head to the kitchen which is why the voice that greets me catches me off guard.

So off guard I'm sure my heart stops beating inside my chest.

"Hello Wren."

The English accent has goose bumps crawling over my skin, the very same voice that spoke to me as I bled out in his arms. The very one that I was sure was going to be the continuation of my suffering and yet turned out to be the very opposite.

My eyes clash with Kingston's, the icy blue a cold that appears too warm, a contrast and contradiction given the circumstances.

"You."

I knew he was coming. I knew he would be back and yet seeing him here, in the flesh is something else entirely.

My memory serves me well in remembering him, even with all the shit that has fallen between us, the tattoos, the casual and yet dangerous demeanor he wears around him as if it were a cloak.

His fingers turn a crystal tumbler of amber liquid on the table, and he leans casually back in the chair, spreading his knees as he looks at me with a smirk.

"I expected a better reception for the man who saved you."

Lex growls beside him, slamming his glass down so hard on the table the crystal cracks, allowing a steady flow of golden liquid to seep from the splices.

"Now, now, Silver," Kingston chuckles, "your woman

does not interest me."

"Well, you did try to fucking buy her."

"Have we not gone over this?" Kingston sighs, "It was for you, I needed an in and she was it. Valentine is just a fucking idiot. Who sells their own fucking daughter?"

A pair of heels clicking on hardwood draws my attention from the man sat at the table. Isobel saunters in, holding a flute of champagne, her jet black hair dead straight and hanging around her face. Pale skin and blood red lips are the first things I notice and then it's the blue of her eyes, so similar to Kingston's.

"Oh!" She beams at me, "look at you!"

She heads right for me and before she can even reach me there is a flurry of activity, bodies jumping up, intercepting hers from mine and then there's Lex, forcing himself in front of me, holding me to his back with one arm whilst his other pulls at the Glock he has concealed.

Kingston, all the while just leans back in his chair and tucks his hands behind his head, grinning. As if this is the funniest thing to happen to him in a while.

"Well," he comments, "A little touchy aren't we, my sister here is just very fond of Wren."

"Your sister needs to back the fuck up!" Ryker threatens, I hadn't noticed him come up on my other side, teeth bared.

189

"It's okay," I say, "I trust her."

And it was true.

I didn't believe she would hurt me, there was something about her, something seriously unhinged, something *dark* but I truly believed that darkness stemmed to something else entirely.

Lex looks to me, I see the confliction, but I also know he wants to give me my own say, my own rule and when I plead him with my eyes, beg him in a way that will only ever be between the two of us he sighs heavily and stands taller, straightening himself and forcing himself to relax a little though he doesn't put the gun away.

"At ease," he orders.

The men around me straighten, tucking their weapons away, all but Ryker and Lex. They sit, though they keep their weapons in view at all times. Isobel cocks a brow, looking at each and every one individually before she huffs and shrugs her shoulder, continuing towards me. Her hands cup my face the moment she is within touching distance, and she stares at me intently, eyes bouncing between mine, "So much fire."

"Hello."

She grins, her teeth a stark contrast to the red staining her lip.

"I am so happy to see you well, Wren."

My brows draw down, there was something about this

woman, something that didn't scream *off,* but unusual. It didn't feel unsafe, but I was also starting to understand that people in this life, they wear many faces.

"Heart," Lex barks, "tell me why you are here."

I cock my head, it appears I arrived right at the nick of time. I wanted to know exactly what it was that Kingston desired.

24

I didn't fucking like this at all.

Heart grins, eyes on his sister and Wren but then slowly moving them to me. "The Syndicate."

My teeth clamp tightly together, the muscle in my jaw aching, "What about them?"

"Well, it appears you have some information on them, I want it."

I scoff, "I have fuck all."

"That's not true, now is it?" Heart licks his teeth, his glass of whiskey dangling between his fingers before he throws the liquid down his throat and pulls out a cigarette, placing it between his lips where it just dangles there.

My mind whirls back to Ainsley. I have no fucking idea if she is even still alive, I haven't heard from her in weeks. She has or at least *had* the information but where it is, I had no fucking idea.

"You're referring to Ainsley," I lean back in my chair.

"I am," he confirms, "she got into the Syndicates servers just before we managed to breach it, downloaded everything. The breach alerted them, and they locked it down before we could get anything, but I know your girl got that info. I want it."

"Why?"

"Let's just say the Syndicate have a lot to pay for," he growls, eyes flicking to his sister who still appears to be infatuated with Wren, cooing and touching her hair. Wren looks at ease with the attention if not a little confused, but Isobel wasn't a threat to her, probably to me and the other men in this room but not Wren.

It wasn't a secret her distaste for men in general though no one knew why exactly.

"Well, Ainsley is not around at the moment," I tell Heart, "Though, should she come through with the information, I'll have a copy sent to you."

"That's not really going to work for me, Alexander," Heart says, lighting the cigarette between his lips.

My eyes narrow, "And what'll happen if I can't provide it?"

His eyes flick to Wren and before anyone can even move or even so much as blink, I have my gun at his temple with the safety off. "I wouldn't even let the thought cross your mind, Heart."

"A deal is a deal, Lex," he turns, not an ounce of fear in his eyes as he stares at me, "I did you a favor, you owe me, if you cannot pay up, do you not think it fair I take back what I gave you?"

I hear his men levelling their guns at me, at Ryker but not at Wren, my own men preparing for a fight that cannot happen.

"You shoot me, Lex, I get her anyway, my men will snatch her right from your grasp and ship her off to somewhere you'll *never* find, even if I'm dead."

"I thought you weren't interested."

"Can we all stop talking like I'm not in the room!?" Wren snaps, stepping away from Isobel to come closer to me.

"Stay where you are!" I order.

"Fuck you, Lex, Kingston, you're asking for something we don't have."

"Then get it," he snaps, "I don't care how you fucking do it, I want that information!"

Isobel sighs heavily and dramatically, throwing herself into a vacant chair at the table. She snatches the bottle of whiskey from the table and unscrews the cap, sipping directly from the bottle.

"You boys want to get your dicks out?" She smiles manically, licking the whiskey from her lips, "Someone grab me a ruler, we can settle this."

Wren pinches the bridge of her nose before she curls her delicate hand around my forearm and begins to push down, trying to get me to stand down.

"This won't do anything but start a war, Lex," she whispers.

She was right. Reluctantly, I drop my weapon and haul her to me, tucking her against my chest.

"Bloody hell," Isobel huffs, "Do you wanna piss on her too? Make sure everyone knows that she is yours? Kingston, stop being a fucking arse, we didn't come here to fight."

King grunts and waves a hand, his guys following his silent order to stand down.

"Look mate, we're not going to take your girl, regardless, the skin trade is not something I'm interested in. I need the information on the syndicate, Ainsley has it."

"When she turns back up, I can give it to you."

"Ainsley will come through," Ryker pipes up.

"She fucking better," Heart growls, "until she does I think I might stick around a while. Brookeshill is quite delightful." His words are dripping in sarcasm, tongue laced in venom. He was a fucking piece of work.

"Little bird," I lean down and whisper to Wren, "Go upstairs, wait for me there."

Her head snaps back. "I don't think so."

Isobel laughs.

"Don't push me, Wren, please, I'll be happier if you were away from this fucking mess."

She wants to fight me, I know she does but ultimately she backs down even if she is far from happy about it.

"Why don't you show me around?" Isobel suggests, standing from the table.

"Leave the bottle," Kingston demands.

Isobel flips him off as she saunters from the room, holding the bottle with Wren trudging behind her, grumbling under her breath.

When the girls are gone, I sit across the table from Kingston, "I haven't heard from Ainsley in weeks."

"She's alive." Is all King says.

"And you know this how?" I ask.

"Your girl is good," he says, "but not that good, we tracked her down in Chicago a few days ago, I have men watching her."

"So why not get the information yourself?" I snap. It was a bluff, I needed that information as much as he did.

"You think she'll just hand it over?"

That was true.

"I mean I can force it if you wish but I don't make it a habit to hurt women."

"Don't you fucking touch her!" Ryker roars.

I slap my hand on his chest, a warning to shut the fuck up. Kingston smirks.

"I've got no problem with you Silver, in fact," Heart leans forward, placing his elbows on the table, "I respect the fuck out of you and your family. It's not often one family can keep reign over a city for the amount of time you have but unfortunately, our two families have now become linked, you have what I need so I gave you what you wanted."

"Wren."

"Women, ay?" He laughs, "weak spots."

I scoff my laughter.

"I'll give you what you need, Heart but I can't do so until Ainsley pulls through."

"I won't be going anywhere." Heart pulls his phone from his pocket, "I'll get someone to pass a message to your girl, anything you want me to say?"

That damn smirk on his face was fucking infuriating, second to the fact that he had connections I didn't know about and means to do it in my fucking city.

"Yeah," I stand, "tell her to get the fuck home, she's needed."

A sudden scream follows my sentence, "Get the fuck down!" Is all I hear before a loud boom shakes the house.

25.
Wren

"This place is gaudy," Isobel comments, swiping a single red fingernail over the frame of a painting hanging on the wall before her eyes drop to the fur rug lining the corridor.

She wasn't necessarily wrong. I don't answer her and have no intentions of showing her around either, I feel like the only reason she offered was to get away from the tension and testosterone saturating the air in the kitchen. I couldn't blame her but I was fucking pissed at Lex.

He forced me into this life, into his world of bloodshed, violence and danger and yet the first sign of trouble he's ushering me out of the room like I'm a precious doll.

I'm not precious and I'm not a doll. I may have been innocent before but that girl no longer exists. If he wanted me at his side then he had to have me there a hundred percent.

I wouldn't be a delicate woman on his arm or a piece of ass people can look at, I'll be just as fierce as he, maybe not as ruthless but I'd have people whispering my name and turning to watch me like he has.

"Hey, what's that?" Isobel draws me from my musings, and I turn to look at where she's peering out the window, looking down the long drive to where the gates are.

I thought it pretty self-explanatory, I mean they're only gates so I cross the hall and look out the window, "That's just –" oh fuck.

A car is barreling down the drive, the gravel kicking up behind the tires. They weren't slowing down and instead of following the drive around they continue over the lawn, cutting huge trenches into the garden, heading right for the kitchen.

Shit.

I grab Isobel's arm and push her towards one of the back rooms before I sprint back towards the kitchen, not caring where she lands or if I hurt her.

"Get the fuck down!" I scream just as the car smashes through a wall in the house.

I dive to the left, my body smashing against the table, my head colliding with the wall as I slump to the floor. The impact isn't too far from me, and I can see the headlights of the car, lights shining through the dust raining all around me.

My ears ringing, I vaguely hear doors slamming and then feet on the ground but it isn't that, that pulls me from the fog in my head trying to drag me down, it's the sound of a scream so filled with terror is turns my blood cold.

Rory.

I had no idea what the fuck was going on, but I could guess who had orchestrated this and there was no fucking way I was going back to my father.

I shakily climb to my feet, covering my nose and mouth in the crook of my elbow and duck around the corner, watching two guys step through the rubble, weapons drawn. They don't even try to come this way, instead head right for the kitchen where Lex and the rest of the guys are.

Idiots.

Rory continues to scream but I know I can't go to her yet, instead I follow behind the two attackers, quietly approaching and staying out of sight as they prepare to enter the kitchen.

Gun shots start ringing, loud bangs that make my head pulse and ears ring even more and a flurry of movement keeps me pinned to the wall, trying to be as silent and still as possible for fear of a gun being turned on me. I've been shot once, it wasn't fun.

One guy goes down whilst the other continues to shoot wildly into the room, shots being fired back but the only thought flowing through my head was that this guy couldn't die.

He was employed by Valentine.

And I need Valentine.

With the loud pops of the gunfire I'm able to creep up on the guy undetected, lifting a large China vase from the ground I raise it above my head as high as I can and smash it down with all the force my body can muster, slamming it around the back of his head hard enough for the vase to shatter into a million pieces, scattering amongst the rubble and stone littering the floor from the destroyed wall.

The guy hits the deck hard and then the gun fire ceases and all eyes turn to me.

Kingston is the first to snap out of it, storming to where the guy lays in the dust, a steady stream of blood seeping from the gash in the back of his head. He's still breathing at least.

Kingston has every intention of shooting the guy and making that breathing stop.

"No!" I scream, jumping forward, "You can't fucking kill him!"

"Why the fuck not!" Kingston bellows.

"Because we need him to find Valentine!"

"Get him in the fucking barn!" Lex orders, rushing towards me to check me over. A few scrapes and bruises but I'll live. Isobel limps towards us, not because she's injured but because she appears to be missing a shoe but other than that she doesn't have a single hair out of place.

What the actual fuck!?

With all the chaos now over, the screaming from upstairs travels through the halls, reminding me that I needed to get to Rory.

I rush to the stairs but two arms band around my waist, hauling me back. Lex's breathing is heavy and hard in my ear, fanning my hair until it tickles against my skin and then Ryker pushes past, taking the stairs two at a time.

"Let him deal with this!" Lex growls.

"Get the fuck off me Lex." I snap. "Stop fucking telling me what to do!"

His hand comes around my throat, holding me further back on him, his fingers squeezing my windpipe, "Little bird," he rasps, "Let's not play fucking games."

"I'm not fucking playing," its hard to speak with his hand on my throat and even despite the current situation, being in this position with him, his dominance and need to control leaves a heat in its wake, one that reminds me every fucking day how fucked I am for this man.

But Rory needs me, and I can revisit this shit later.

I slam an elbow back into his stomach, shocking him enough for him to let me go and before he can grab me again, I dart to the stairs, too quick for him to catch me. I climb the stairs to his curses, joined by a chorus of laughter from Kingston and his sister.

"Shit, Silver, you got yourself a wild one," Kingston's voice becomes distant the higher in the house I get.

"No! I can't go back!" I hear as I round the corner on the hall, my feet slipping on the hardwood. "I can't go back."

"Put the gun down, Rory, you're not going back."

My heart sinks.

On shaky legs I make it to the door and tug at the handle, pulling and pulling but the thing doesn't fucking open.

"Open the door!" I scream.

Lex is at the end of the hall, storming towards me, his face a mask of pure rage but I don't give a fuck about that, he can be angry later.

"I can't," she sobs. "I can't go back, you don't understand."

"Will you shoot me?" Ryker asks.

My heart sinks further.

"Put the gun down."

"You're going to send me back."

"Rory!" Ryker shouts.

"I'm not going back!"

"No!" Ryker booms.

Rory's scream is followed by a gun shot.

Both Lex and I freeze, the air being sucked from my lungs.

The thud of a body hitting the floor makes me jump.

She shot him.

She shot Ryker.

26.

Wren begins to pound on the door, throwing her whole body weight against the wood but the thing doesn't budge.

"Rory!" she screams, "open the fucking door."

Shock and anger course through my system, "Move." I order.

She does as she is told, moving to the left as I position myself in front of the door and kick it, once, twice, hearing the wood crack and splinter under the force, on the third kick the thing swings open. I don't enter straight away, I push Wren behind my body and withdraw my gun, entering with it leveled ahead of me and ready to be used.

She fucking shot Ryker.

The smell of blood, metallic and coppery permeates the

air of the room and I find Ryker on his knees, leaning forward with blood pooling in front of him.

Only when I step further in, it isn't his blood staining the carpet, but Aurora's.

She lays in the middle of the floor, a hole in her temple where she turned the gun on herself.

"I couldn't stop her."

A scream lashes through the room, as sharp as a whip, "no, no, no," Wren sobs, dropping down beside her friend, knees hitting the puddle of crimson seeping out the side of Aurora's head, "Call an ambulance!"

"Little bird," I try. There was no coming back from this.

"Call a fucking ambulance!"

"She's dead, Wren." Ryker says.

"No!" Wren manically shakes her head, pressing her hands to the wound as if that'll somehow bring her back. "She's not, she can't be."

Sobs make her voice quake and she sucks in air, trying to fill her lungs as grief robs her of oxygen. Her face is crumpled, eyes wide and pleading, tears streaking down her cheeks.

Closing my eyes, I sigh.

"Little bird," I soothe, stepping behind her to rest my hand on her shoulder, smoothing her sweat dampened hair away from her forehead.

She collapses back against my legs, blood coating her hands and arms and legs and she screams. Her cry hits me straight to the soul, earth shattering and grief stricken in a way I have never and will never want to experience.

Her pure, unfiltered emotion feels as if it'll shatter windows, her cries no doubt heard throughout the house. No one comes though, not Kingston, not Isobel, knowing when to interfere and when not to.

Carefully, I drag Wren from the floor, holding her to me as she buries her face into my chest and continues to cry. Bloody handprints stain my shirt, dirt and ash mixing with the crimson. She lets me guide her from the room and I signal for Ryker to get some men in here to clean this up before I shut us away in our bedroom.

She doesn't make it to the bed, instead choosing to sit in the middle of the carpet, bringing her knees to her chest as if to contain everything inside of her. She wraps her arms around her legs, holding on tight as she rocks, staring vacantly at a spot on the wall.

"Let's get this blood off you," I say to her, "Okay?"

She nods once, mute and follows me to the bathroom, stripping from her blood drenched clothes which land with a wet slap onto the tiles and then she steps into shower before the water has even warmed. The water sliding from her skin is tinged red, circling at her feet before it drains down the plug, but she continues to stare at the wall, arms limp at her sides, letting the water hit her.

I don't undress as I climb in with her, turning the temperature up a bit further to try and rid her of the goose bumps that have taken purchase on her skin. I help wash the blood from her skin, my clothes sticking to my body but she doesn't appear to be here, stuck inside her head.

When she's cleaned, I guide her out, wrap her in a towel and sit her on the bed. I'll do everything if I need to.

"He did this." She says as I come back from the wardrobe with a fresh pair of leggings and one of my shirts.

"Valentine," she affirms, eyes finally meeting mine. "This is his fault."

I nod.

"Where is the guy?" She asks. "The one from earlier."

"In the barn."

I wait for the wince, the grimace, but it never comes.

"I want to come."

"Wren–"

"No!" She snaps, cutting me off. "I let you push me out that room earlier. I let you do that but you want me here, you have to let me in. I'm not going to fucking sit in this little cage you've built for me, I'm in or I am not."

"It's not that simple." I growl.

"Then make it that simple!"

She sighs, stepping up to me, her eyes clouded and misty, tears still making her eyes watery, "I fell in love with you. You. Despite the shit you do and the blood on your hands. You fucking kidnapped me and yet I still fucking love you. How fucked up is that!" she laughs, "You're a twisted, ruthless motherfucker, Alexander and I'm still fucking here."

I swallow.

"Let me fucking in. Teach me."

This was a bad fucking idea.

"Wren," I try once more.

"Alexander."

She wasn't budging. There was no movement, no negotiation. Anyone else, there wouldn't even be the time of day, her, I'll give her everything. What was it Kingston said? Weak spots. Like showing a predator your jugular.

There was no doubt she was that one spot that'll kill me before anything else and everyone knows it.

How can I protect her if she's there with me? My enemies would use her to hurt me, would take her and ruin her and break her just to get to me.

"I can't be a pawn anymore," she says so quietly, "I can't do nothing anymore."

I drop my head, "Fine."

There's no celebration, no eager thanks because she may as well have signed our death certificates.

"After tonight, we're moving," I tell her, handing her the clothes.

She puts them on.

"Where?"

"I take it you're opposed to moving to a safe house?" I try.

She glares at me.

"The penthouse in the city."

"Okay."

When she is dressed, she pulls her wet hair into a ponytail, her hands shaking but she's pushed all that grief behind a mask of determination. She wants Valentine's destruction and she'll do anything to get it.

"You don't have to do this," I tell her, sliding my hand into hers.

"Yes, I do."

She doesn't look at me, but her hand holds mine in a tight grip, palm sweaty and a tremble in her fingers. She's afraid.

I squeeze her hand and force us to stop in the hall, pinning her suddenly to a wall. Caged between my arms, she stares up at me, my sweet little bird with glassy green eyes and a somber look on her face.

I feather my fingers down her face, unable to get enough of her. Her eyes flutter closed beneath the touch, lashes flickering against the apples of her cheeks and she leans in to my hand.

"I will always protect you," I tell her, "You will always be first."

"Your city comes first," she breathes, pressing a kiss to my palm.

"Not anymore, little bird."

Her eyes open and she stares up at my face, checking for deceit in my words but she'll find none. I never thought it possible. Weakened by a woman, brought to my knees by a single female who started out as a means to an end but became my queen instead.

"I love you," I whisper against her mouth.

She melts into me, fusing her lips to mine.

When the kiss turns heated and my cock grows hard, pushing against her lower belly I pull away. There could be no distractions with what is to come tonight. I needed to have my head in the game, I needed to protect Wren and get what we both needed to end this once and for all.

Her teeth drag against my lower lip, and she spears me

with a glare, "let's go."

"After you, little bird."

27.

Wren

The first thing that hits me is the smell.

Blood, sweat and piss all mingle together to create a stench so heady it makes me gag. I wretch, my stomach cramping and my throat constricting.

"You don't have to do this," Lex calmly states again, placing his hand on my spine to soothe me.

But I did have to do this, for if I am to stand by his side I need to be just as formidable and ruthless, someone not to be fucked with no matter how delicate I may look.

I inhale through my mouth rather than my nose, pushing down the need to vomit and straighten. My chin tilts up and I steel my spine.

This is for Rory. For me. For Lex's mother. For all the women Valentine has hurt and tortured.

I drag my eyes across the dusty floor of the barn, noticing the dark spots that are forever stained into the ground. Blood. This is what this city lives on, thrives on it. Blood and pain and corruption.

And I am now sitting beside the king of chaos himself.

The man I had hit over the head earlier dangles from a hook suspended from a beam in the ceiling of the barn, arms chained with steel above his head. He's been stripped to his boxers and blood covers every available inch of his body, there's barely any skin showing through the crimson paint covering him. His head hangs, chin to chest and his eyes are closed though his chest moves with each labored breath that wheezes through his lungs.

Ryker stands to the side, a hammer of some sort dangling from his hand and blood splatters over his face and arms, staining his white shirt. His eyes are dead. Void of any emotion and it's the first time I realize he's just as formidable as the man next to me.

He doesn't seem as ruthless but with the almost satisfied and content look he holds on his face, he appears to be enjoying the torture.

His eyes meet mine and he nods his head.

"Well, well, well," Lex steps away from me, "What do we have here?" The voice, the demeanor, it's like nothing I have ever experienced with him. He holds himself differently, his voice not even slightly resembling the one I heard back in the hall as he declared his love for me. "A Valentine rat."

The guy in chains startles, the steel links clanging

together loudly, echoing through the barn and spooking a couple of rats that had been hiding behind some cabinets on the back wall. They scurry out, darting from their safe shadows for safer spots outside.

I had always wondered what this barn looked like. Worn and depleted from the outside and that was exactly how it was on the inside. Bare walls, dirty floor and a few rusty and old tables scattered around the space, holding a variety of weapons, from daggers to hacksaws. There's a couple of chairs laying about but not enough to hold a party.

"Kill me and get it over with." The guys spits.

"Oh no," Lex wags his finger, "When is it ever that easy?"

The guy curls his lip, eyes bouncing between him and Ryker before his evil gaze lands on me.

His bloodshot eyes do a once over on my body and then another only slower, following each line and curve of my body until he reaches my face and curls back his lip, "such a shame Valentine wouldn't let us have a taste of your pretty little cunt."

I stifle the need to recoil. I am not afraid of him.

His head snaps back so suddenly and so hard I'm amazed his neck doesn't break but he drapes forward, blood dribbling from his mouth as he laughs, "May as well let her go now, Silver, she won't be yours forever."

Another hit.

The guy laughs.

"I imagined what it would be like," he heaves, "to taste that pretty little pussy."

He was taunting Lex, forcing his hand, making him lose his cool enough for him to snap and kill the guy. It was what he wanted, and he was getting exactly that. With each word uttered against me, Lex's patience and anger was waning thin.

"I wanted to know if she would scream or lay there silently, accepting her fate. Tell me, Silver, is her pussy tight like I imagined? Does it feel like heaven when you sink into her body? Does she scream?"

Lex tenses beside me but I quickly grasp his arm before he strikes.

"I watched her, bloody and broken and beaten," the guy taunts, "I imagined what it would be like to sink inside that sweet body as I pressed on her windpipe. I could picture the way her eyes bulged and she fought me as I choked her to death and fucked her like the simple little fucking woman she is."

Lex's muscles are so rigid and coiled, it's only a matter of time before he snaps again.

I pretend to be horrified at the words and whilst they *are* repulsive, I find them not nearly as terrifying as they should be. He didn't do it because he is simply a dog. Following orders. Always following orders. He wants Lex to kill him, so he doesn't talk and using me is the quickest way to get there.

Feigning terror, I bury myself into Lex's neck which instinctively has his arm coming around me in a protective embrace, trying to shield me from the darkness.

Doesn't he know he introduced me to it. He whispered in my ear and called me forth. And I answered. I was always going to answer.

"He is baiting you," I whisper so faintly I worry he may not hear.

When his fingers dig into my flesh, I know he heard my message.

The guy continues anyway and risking a glance over my shoulder I see his eyes perusing my body like I'm a prime cut of meat waiting to be eaten.

"Fuck," he smirks, "let me have a taste before I die," he says, "Just show me that cunt, dripping. Make it wet for me, let me imagine what she might taste like."

"You want to see her wet?" Lex asks, finally understanding. A calm wave washes over his face, relaxing his features and schooling his expression. Gone is the rage, the fire burning in his eyes, replaced by blissful indifference.

My eyes squeeze shut. I hated this. It made me sick, but I knew it had to be done.

"Yes."

Lex feathers his fingers down my side before releasing

me, ushering me back as he advances on the guy hanging from the ceiling.

"That, unfortunately, is not on the table," Lex says, "You been in this game long?"

"A while."

"Then you should know that *my wife* is a no go for scum like you."

"Your wife?" the guy scoffs. "You married the tramp?"

"Mm-hmm," Lex nods, lying but I would be a fool if I didn't like being called his wife. "So, let's strike a deal, shall we? You tell me what I want to know and I'll make it quick."

"Fuck you."

"Where is Valentine!?"

"Torture me all you want, I'll never talk."

Lex holds out his hand and someone places a thin steel blade in his palm. The handle is leather bound, black with a single strip of white material that wraps around the hilt and has a dangling silver emblem hanging from the knot. I can't make out what it is from here but whatever it is, Lex thumbs it lovingly and I can only assume it holds value.

Alexander suddenly plunges forward, burying the thin blade into the abdomen of the prisoner and he wails, blood pouring from the wound and covering Lex's hand.

"Where. Is. Valentine."

When the guy quiets he snatches the blade from his stomach, wiping it on the dark material of his pants.

"Fuck you, Silver."

"I'm in!" A sudden yell from a guy I hadn't even realized was in the same room as us, fills the space and Lex's grin is telling. It's menacing and corrupt and bloodthirsty.

Ryker steps up next to me, a huge presence but I don't feel unsafe around him as he presses his hand to my shoulder and squeezes, his silent condolences for Rory. But it was more than that too, it was his way of showing me he was here. He had my back. I had his protection.

I am glad he didn't die.

I am glad she didn't shoot him, but I would have preferred neither of them being hurt.

Her death makes my gut churn, the sadness, the sorrow makes everything inside me hurt. I should have saved her. I should have done more but she died anyway. Permanently erased from the world and with her death, I lost a little bit of light.

A cell phone is pressed into Lex's palm by a guy I've never seen before and then he scurries from the room.

"Do you know what I have here?" Lex asks.

I'm impressed. Despite his injuries, the blood seeping

from various wounds, the bruises blooming on his skin, the guy stands tall, head held high and he shows no fear.

Lex holds up the cell phone, "Last message. Received at seven twenty three today," He mocks a cough to clear his throat, 'let me know when it is done. Wire transfer ready.' By someone named V. That doesn't happen to be Valentine, now does it?"

The guy stays quiet.

"It's okay," Lex shrugs, "I don't need you anymore."

I don't have time to grasp the meaning of his words before he pulls out his gun and shoots the guy in the chest.

The guys eyes bug out of his head and his head angles down to look at the wound in his chest. Blood spurts and dribbles from the wound, streaming over his skin like a leak in a tap.

And then he is dead. Gone.

Like he never existed at all.

Lex turns to me, the gun still dangling from his fingertips, "We have him little bird." Fingers trail down the side of my face, "It's time you have your vengeance."

28

Wren's face remains impassive, no emotion showing there but her eyes give her away. Shock. A little fear but she inhales a deep breath, closes her eyes and when she reopens them, she looks at the dead man like he is nothing but a doll.

Good girl.

She leans into my hand as I put the gun away and then I'm hauling her to me, slamming my mouth onto hers. She kisses me back, hard, rough, teeth scraping and biting. The copper tang of blood hits my tongue from where she split my lip with her bite and then she licks it clean, soothing the sting.

Holy fucking shit.

"Let's go," I tell her, needing her away from this place and alone with me.

I leave the guys to clean up and walk back to the destroyed house, a draft blowing in through the smashed wall. King is still in the kitchen, his legs up on the table as he takes a puff of his cigarette, a bottle of whiskey dangling from the fingers of his other hand, "Shame about the wall." He comments. I narrow my eyes on him, noting the thin trickle of blood now dried on the side of his brow.

He's going to drive me insane before I've got the information from Ainsley. I pack a small suitcase for Wren and me whilst she sits on the bed, watching me move through the room, collecting things. I don't take much, just the essentials for the time being, anything else can be purchased. With a bag and my little bird, I head to the garage, guiding Wren to the passenger side of the Maserati.

She runs a finger down the side and smirks at me, "nice ride."

I grin and open the door, watching her climb in, green eyes stalking me.

Justice is so close I can taste it on my tongue. Ryker will give the cell to one of our tech guys who'll trace Valentine and then once I have his location, we'll strike.

There's no games this time, as soon as I have him in my sights, he's dead.

It feels like years since I've been at the penthouse though everything is exactly how I left it. Plush grey carpets, white walls save for the left side of the apartment which is just glass looking down onto the city below. We are far enough up that we don't get the noise of the streets below, no traffic or loud sirens, just a gentle whistle of the wind as it blows passed the glass. I place the bags in the corridor and hit the house service button, they'll prepare the bedroom and put away our belongings before disappearing again. Everyone in this building is here because I deemed it so, the staff, the residents.

Wren is looking at everything and nothing at all, eyes sweeping over the plush interior, the couches and bars. It's modern and sleek, lavish with the marble units and large leather sectional positioned in front of an open fire.

I head to the bar and pull out a bottle of whiskey and two tumblers, running them beneath some water to rid them of any dust before I throw in some ice and pour the amber liquid over the top, the frozen cubes cracking as the fluid hits them.

Wren stops at the windows, leaning over to press a button that allows the panes to slide open to a balcony. She steps out onto the slate tiles and places her hands on the rails, peering down at my kingdom. *Our* kingdom.

"The city seems so different up here," she murmurs, voice almost swallowed by the wind, but I hear her.

I place the drinks on the table to the right and step up behind her, pressing her into the rails.

"Different how?"

"Like it isn't full of men with too much power and not riddled with corruption."

I grin against her neck, stifling the need to sink my teeth into her throat as she angles her head to the side to allow me better access.

My cock presses into her ass and my hands grip the railing beside hers. "Do you like it?" I ask.

"Mm," she breathes, pressing back harder.

Shit.

I spin her so she's facing me, wild hair being teased by the wind and make quick work at ridding her of her clothes. Goosebumps chase across her skin, nipples puckering in the cold.

"You look so beautiful with the kingdom at your feet," I rasp, sliding a finger over the mound of her breast. If the cold bothers her she doesn't show it, instead she arches her spine, pushing her chest out for my palm to squeeze. "So fucking beautiful."

I continue my way down her body, slipping between her legs to rub the pad of my finger over her clit, finding her wet and ready for me. Always so ready for me.

"All for me," I muse.

"Lex," she moans.

I step forward and lift her, backing up until her ass is on the railing and the thirty floor drop right at her back.

Her eyes bug out of her head and her nails bite into my shoulders, gripping tightly as the fear of falling makes all her muscles tense up.

"Lex!" She screams.

"Yes baby?"

"I'll fall!"

"You think I'd let you fall, little bird?" I step between her legs, holding her tightly as I kiss up her throat.

She whimpers, a mixture of fear and arousal. Her pulse jumps wildly under my lips and her thighs shake but I feel her wetness seeping through the thin material of my shirt.

"Does it scare you to know that it could end at any moment?" I murmur, "That this could be it?"

Her nails bite even harder into my skin but she rolls her hips, rubbing her pussy against me, searching for more.

"Hold on," I tell her with a grin.

I let go and her legs wrap around me, along with her arms, holding on as if I'd ever let her go. If she falls, I'll be going with her.

Using one hand I unbuckle my belt and unbutton my pants, tugging them down until my cock is free. I guide it to the entrance, feeling her warmth envelope me, sheathing my dick as I slide in slowly.

"Does it turn you on to know that death is just one slip away and yet you know it'll never come because I'd never let you fall."

"Alexander," she moans.

"That's it, baby," I pull out and then slide back in, a sweat breaking out across my skin as I pull at my own restraints. "How does it feel to be fucked in front of our entire kingdom?"

Nails biting into my flesh I slam into her, holding her as her body slips further back on the railing. It's dangerous and sexy as fuck, reckless in the most delicious way.

I fuck her with the city at her feet, her body precariously close to the edge and slipping back with each deep thrust. The sound of our skin slapping together is drowned out by the wind but her moans of pleasure echo deep inside my bones.

"Fuck, yes," she cries, "Lex!"

"You like it, little bird?"

"Yes, Lex! Yes!"

My hands bruise her hips as I hold her there, thrusting my hips, fucking her and watching her, eyes closed, mouth parted as she loses herself to the sensations. I watch her breasts move with each thrust and can't help myself as I lean forward and capture one between my teeth.

She cries out, her climax slamming into her full force. Her thighs tighten around me, limiting my movements as she holds me flush to her body, cock buried to the hilt inside as her walls clamp and spasm around me, but I'm not done yet. I need more. When she calms, I help her from the railing and spin her, bending her so her face is over the railing and she's staring down at the street below. One hand on the back of her neck, holding her there, the other squeezes her ass as I slip back inside.

She moans as I bury myself to the hilt and then pull out, slamming forward again, keeping that hand pressed to the back of her neck. I fuck her hard and fast, relentlessly and brutally, slamming into her hard enough that she jerks forward with each thrust but she pushes back all the same, her cries getting louder as she climbs to her next orgasm.

"Come for me, little bird," I tell her, "I want another."

"Yes," she cries as I let go of her hip and reach around, teasing her clit with my fingers.

"There's my little bird," I whisper against her spine, the hand not holding her neck dancing over her body, memorizing each curve and dip and edge, "There's my good girl." I whisper my praise against her flesh, "Are you my good girl, little bird?"

Not waiting for an answer, I straighten, keeping my hand on her neck, slowly withdrawing from her only to slam back home once more, "Look at our city, my love, look at our city whilst I worship its queen."

Her legs wobble as she climaxes once more, drawing my own from me. Her scream is swallowed by the wind and my roar is hollered at the sky. My muscles bunch and tense as I spill into her, her pussy walls squeezing me for every last drop.

We stand there, breathing heavy, bodies sweaty continuing to stare down at our city.

I press a kiss to her spine, "Forever may we rule."

29

I step from the bathroom, my towel wrapped around my hips to find Wren curled up in the middle of our bed. Her hair is damp from her own shower and one of my shirts covers her slim body. She stares towards the wall of windows, looking out at the skyline.

Lights blink on the horizon and right in the distance you can see a cargo ship coming into port.

"What are you thinking?" I ask, dropping the towel to put on a pair of gym shorts before I join her on the bed.

"Rory," she sniffs.

I sigh and run a hand down her spine, "I am sorry about your friend."

"She has a sister," she says, "I guess she'll never know what happened."

"Ryker will take care of it."

"How?"

"He'll think of something."

"She'll just be forgotten, buried like everyone else in this life. It'll be a wound left open, no closure."

"No Little bird, she won't, I'll make sure of it. She will get the burial she deserves."

She inhales deeply and turns to face me, her eyes red rimmed from her recent tears. I wish I could take it away.

I reach forward but my phone ringing loudly from the dresser halts my hand. "Go on." Wren says with a gentle tilt of her lips, staying exactly where she is, so I do, climbing from the bed to pick up the call, keeping my eyes on her.

"Lex." I answer.

"We have him," Ryker says on the other end, his voice rushed and breathless, "pinging you the address now."

My phone buzzes against the side of my head and I pull it away, reading the address, "next city over." I comment.

"When do you want to hit?"

"Tonight, I'm not giving him a chance to move. Get some men, meet at the penthouse in an hour."

I hang up.

Wren is climbing from the bed, throwing the shirt from her body as she searches for different clothing.

"You're not coming," I growl.

"Like fuck I'm not."

"Yeah, what's going to happen if Valentine gets you again, hm? You think he's just going to kidnap you? He'll kill you, Wren."

"Probably the same thing that'll happen to you, Lex," she hollers back.

"Don't fucking push me, this is final. You. Are. Not. Coming."

"Fuck you, Alexander. You leave without me, and I'll find my own way there."

"Wren," I try, lowering my tone, "I can't have you with me."

"You're not taking this from me," she pulls on a pair of leggings and a sweater, "I'm coming."

"And what if something happens to you?"

I hated this. I fucking hated it.

"Give me a gun and a knife. I'll be fine."

I lick my teeth, narrowing my eyes, "Tell me little bird, are you prepared to shoot a man?"

"I shot you," she fires back.

"But not to kill," I retaliate, "You shot me yes, but you couldn't kill me. You couldn't kill the man that kidnapped you. Hurt you. Kept you in his house. You couldn't end the one life that would have stopped this whole thing."

"That's different."

"Valentine is your father."

"No, he is not." She snaps as she tilts her chin up, staring at me, "I am *not* a Valentine."

"A Lawson?" I say.

"No."

"Then what?"

She stomps her way towards me, my very own little ball of fury, she stabs her finger into my chest, "I am a fucking Silver."

Hearing her say it makes my cock jerk in my pants. Holy fucking shit.

I push away the burning desire to seal that fate and say, "How can you be sure you'll put a bullet in his head if the time called for it?"

"I want to see his heart, Lex. That man deserves to die. I want to do it."

I curl a finger beneath her chin, pressing a kiss to her lips, "I don't want you there, baby."

"You don't have a choice."

"There's always a choice."

"Not this time."

I sigh and cross the room, pulling out a box from beneath the bed. Inside is a handgun, small and light and I hand it to her, along with a box of ammo. "This was my mothers. Her preferred weapon of choice."

Wren weighs it in her hand and then tucks it into the back of her leggings.

I pull out a knife next, a dagger of sorts with a leather hilt and a sharp as fuck blade that glints in the low lighting of the room and hand it to her.

"Don't cut yourself," I grin.

She presses the tip of it against the side of my throat, the point nicking my skin enough for blood to well quickly and roll down the side of my neck.

"This'll do." She smirks.

I wipe the blood with my palm and cock a brow as she leans forward and licks it from my fingers, "Let's go."

Fucking damn siren.

Ryker climbs from the front seat and hops in the back as I climb behind the wheel and Wren slides into the front.

"Thirty minutes east," Ryker says from behind, "guys are en route."

"We kill him," I tell him, "No hesitation."

"Yes boss."

"Hi Gruff," Wren looks back at him, peering between the two seats. In the mirror I see him raise a brow and shake his head. "How's the nose?"

"Healed but sore."

She laughs turning back around and settling against the chair before turning her face to the window to watch the city roll by.

I reach across and squeeze her thigh, the shape of her legs clearly visible with the tight fitting pants, "Are you sure you're ready for this?"

"Never been more ready."

About ten minutes from our destination, Ryker passes something to Wren between the seats and with a frown she takes it, staring down at the piece of paper between her fingers.

I risk a glance over to find a picture of Wren and Rory,

dressed in bikinis in front of a swimming pool. It appears to be somewhere abroad though I can't tell where exactly, but they look…happy.

Wren's fingers flex on the image, "Where did you get this?"

"I guess when Valentine took Rory, she had a handbag or something, one of Heart's men retrieved this from a bunch of other personal belongings they found in the house."

"We were in Egypt," she says, "a year ago now."

"I'm sorry, Wren. I tried," Ryker says.

"I know," she answers. "it's not your fault."

Wren stares down at the image for a little bit longer before she tucks it into the glove compartment and steels herself, lifting her chin and pushing back the emotion that I can see trying to force its way out.

That's my girl.

Was I worried? Of course I fucking was, but I had to give this to her.

I squeeze her thigh once more before returning both hands to the steering wheel and stopping a few streets down from our destination.

There's a number of dark SUVs lining the street, my men. When I climb out, they all do too and to my surprise, Kingston and a few of his men join us.

"Heart," I greet.

"You didn't think I'd miss out on all the fun, did you?" He grins.

"No Isobel?" Wren asks.

"She's a little busy," he says, eyeing her. "I'm sorry about your friend." He says to her gently, showing a side to him I didn't think existed.

She nods and swallows, curling her fingers into the palms of her hand. With a final look at her he turns to me, nodding once.

"Kill everyone," I tell them, "no prisoners. No survivors."

That's the only plan. I don't care how it is done, but they're all meeting the reaper tonight.

30

The building anxiety within my body makes my hands shake, I'd like to say I am not afraid of Valentine, but I'd also be lying. Of course, the man scares me, the things he did, the things I heard, there's no going back from that.

We walk silently towards the destination, a row of guys in front and a number behind and Lex never lets go of my hand. The building comes into view, an abandoned motel by the looks of it, deserted and run down with the old sign hanging from a pole.

Litter and debris is scattered across the parking lot, being disturbed by the gentle breeze but other than that, it is quiet. No lights shine from within the depleted building, no sign of life and for a minute I doubt the intel Lex has received.

Was Valentine even here?

Was it a trap?

Lex silently orders his men to scatter with a flick of his finger and then it's just me, Lex, Ryker and Kingston. I look around, searching for the others but they are out of sight, having merged with the shadows, disappearing. Lex steers me towards what would have been the front entrance of the building.

The front doors are off their hinges, dangling from the frame and Ryker moves one aside so we can enter. Inside smells like rotting wood and dust, a stifling smell that makes my throat close up and eyes water.

"Wren," Lex hisses, "behind me, Ryker and King take that hall."

I don't say a single word as they follow his orders, vanishing down a long, dingy hall way that cuts sharply right and I drop in behind Lex, following blindly down a corridor that's darker than the pits of hell.

It's silent between us other than the steady rate of our breathing but a slight creak in a door frame to the left has my feet pausing on the threadbare carpet. Lex doesn't hear it but I do.

I pause, turning my head towards the sound, my brows pulling low.

I can hear Lex walking further and further away from me but I'm so focused on this sound that I can't help myself, like sleeping beauty drawn to the spindle, I turn and make my way towards the source of the noise.

A barely there glow from beneath a door has my hackles rising.

I know, I *know*, Valentine is there.

I press my hand to the handle, prepared to push down but a sudden body behind mine stops me.

"Hello, daughter," Valentine's rancid breath huffs passed my nose as his hand comes around my throat, pressing the edge of a blade to my windpipe.

I expected to be paralyzed with fear, with dread, with a doom so stifling it would stop my heart, but I just feel *pissed* off.

My nostrils flare and my teeth grit as he steers me away from the door, back towards the corridor where Lex continues to search, the razor edge biting into my skin. He isn't alone either, there's two guys with him, silent with guns drawn, going ahead before the two of us do. Searching for Lex. I swallow, the movement of my throat making the edge of the blade cut into my skin.

The two guys suddenly raise their guns, aiming ahead of them as Lex's footsteps draw closer.

"No!" I scream, knowing they'll shoot first. Lex's steps stop and silence settles around us.

"You stupid bitch," Valentine bellows, pressing the edge in hard enough to cut into my skin. I feel blood rolling down my throat, seeping into the collar of my sweater. "Go," he orders his men, "I want him alive."

They silently obey his order, their steps careful as they advance down the corridor, avoiding the glass and debris scattered across the floor.

Valentine keeps the blade on my throat but moves the other to the back of my head, roughly grabbing a fist full of hair and yanking my head back hard enough I feel my neck crack.

"Move," He hisses, shoving me forward, towards a closed door. "Open it."

I do, nostrils flaring as I try to figure out a way to get the fuck out of his hold without him slicing me open.

Once inside the room he just pushes the door to, leaving it slightly ajar and positions us in the centre, holding me tightly against him, my back to his front. His breathing is heavy and uneven, his heartbeat erratic, giving away his fear. I feel myself smile, just a small tilt of my lips knowing in these last moments he would know nothing but fear.

The silence around us is abruptly shattered with several loud gunshots. The shots echo through the depleted building, bouncing off the crumbling walls and ricocheting inside my head. My heart pounds harder, my fear for Lex making my eyes sting with emotion.

Valentine's hold tightens on me as footsteps begin to approach, a slow and even pace, casual and yet with each thud of their foot, the tension around us seems to get tighter, like a rope is being pulled and any minute it'll snap. Thump. Thump. Thump.

The steps stop outside the door and it feels like minutes pass before anything happens. Valentine's breath puffs chaotically at my ear and even my own increases, wondering what the fuck is about to happen.

The door is pushed, and it opens slowly, so slowly, the hinges creaking and then there he is.

Lex stands in the threshold, eyes wide but not in fear but with a crazed sort of rage that makes everything simmer rather than boil. There are blood spots on his face, on his shirt and his gun dangles loosely in his grip.

His head cocks to the side as he takes us both in, eyes scanning me from my feet, all the way up my body, checking for injury. His eyes snag on the blood on my throat and when he finally meets my eyes, the man I know is no longer there.

No, the man staring back at me is the very one that is whispered on the wind. The devil in this concrete jungle. His eyes slide from me to Valentine slowly, casually.

"Here's what's going to happen," Valentine says, his voice shaking with the fear I can feel pounding against my spine. "You're going to leave. Both here *and* the city, once I know you're gone, I'll send Wren back."

"You believe me stupid, Valentine?" Lex cocks his head again in that way of his that makes him look like a predator sizing up his prey. There is no hate or anger masking is tone, everything about him is just so measured. Easy. Like I don't have a knife held to my throat and he didn't just kill two men.

"You have no choice." Valentine presses the blade harder into my neck and I wince, squeezing my eyes closed.

"Let her go and I might consider not killing you." Lex

says, and my eyes home in on him, pupils blown so wide his eyes appear black.

I hope he's fucking bluffing.

Even so, there was no way I was letting my father leave here alive.

Keeping that blade to my throat, Valentine pulls a gun, aiming it at Lex, "Or *I'll* just kill you both."

Lex is quick to level his own gun, eyes pinging to me where I stay trapped against Valentine, a silent message. *Stay very, very still.*

We stand there for minutes, no one talking, no one moving, "Let her go." Lex growls.

Pain explodes in my right ear, travelling through my skull as a gun is fired right next to my face. It's so sudden, so abrupt Lex just stands there, his brows pulling low whilst blood blooms like a growing rose on the front of his shirt, and then he stumbles, legs barely able to hold him up as he droops and drops to the floor.

He shot him.

"NO!" I scream.

A rage I've never felt before fills my body, turning the blood in my veins to lava as I see red. All my training, every ounce of it comes back to me in a flash and I use it, managing to get Valentine's blade away from my throat. Legs and fists fly as he tries to take back his advantage, all the while, Lex lays there on the ground,

243

moving, trying to get up, his blood dripping onto the carpet.

I kick the gun out of Valentine's hand and he lunges for me, slicing the blade towards me. I dodge the knife, managing to avoid it penetrating but the edge slices across my arm, cutting through the fabric of my sweater and then across my flesh.

The pain barely registers as I rip my own knife out, holding it out in front of me as he circles. My fingers flex on the hilt, I am so ready for this. *I am so ready.*

He lunges forward but I dodge again, managing to come up the side of him and I don't think, only act as I plunge the knife into the side of his throat, straight through the artery and then the windpipe.

My father stills. Blood coats my hand, my arms and the front of my clothing as Valentine drops the blade he was holding to favor holding his throat.

I pull the blade out, watching the blood spurt from the wound, coating me even further.

I thought killing someone like this would do more. I thought I'd feel quilt, sorrow, grief, but all I feel is fucking powerful. I took him. I killed him.

I got my revenge, for me, for Rory and for Lex.

I watch him sink to his knees, his blood spewing down his front and onto the floor. His eyes meet mine, so similar to my own and he reaches forward, fingers curling into the front of my sweater whilst his other hand still holds his throat. He's so weak the tug barely even moves me. I lift my chin, my breaths coming heavy as I look down my nose at where he is dying on his knees in front of me.

I reach down and take his hand, pulling it away from me and stare at him. His mouth forms the word please and I smile, "Goodbye Valentine."

Lifting my leg, I press the sole of my shoe against his chest and kick. He tumbles back, landing with a loud thud into the dirt. I watch the remaining bits of life drain from him, pooling in puddles around his throat.

Dead. Finally fucking dead.

"Little bird," Lex rasps.

My head snaps around and I rush towards him, dropping down to the side and looking for the damage. A bullet hole, straight through the upper section of his shoulder, a through and through. It hasn't hit anything major but there is a lot of fucking blood, but I had to wonder, how much of it actually belonged to him.

"Kiss me." He growls.

I press my hand to the wound and stifle his hiss of breath with my mouth. Both of us covered in blood, Valentine's blood pooling in the dust and the dirt beneath our knees, I kiss him and I don't stop.

His one good arm comes around me, pulling me to his body and I straddle his lap, kissing him harder, deeper, a fiery need taking possession of my body. Adrenaline and lust warms me through and I roll my hips against Lex's growing erection. His blood seeps through my fingers, warm and wet but I still don't stop.

"You did it," Lex breathes against my lips.

"Lex," I moan.

We're both covered in blood, injured, tired and yet I *can't* fucking stop. I need him. I need him now.

"Fuck me," I whisper.

The vibration of his growl travels to the back of my throat and then he's lifting me from his lap to unbutton his pants and pulls them down whilst I do the same with my leggings before I sink onto his rigid length, burying it until I feel him pressing so deep inside me I see stars. Our skin, wet and crimson slides together and I ride him, hard and quick, the need to release stronger than anything I've ever felt.

"You look so fucking beautiful," he growls, eyes a little manic, taking in my blood stained face.

I gyrate my hips, lifting from him only to slam back down again, crying out as my body begins to build for a release.

"Shit," I cry.

"That's it," Lex growls.

My orgasm hits me like a truck, shaking my bones and muscles and forcing me to still on top of him, my head dropping and burying into the crook of his neck, twitching as it rockets through me. Lex doesn't stop though, he lifts me slightly so he can piston his hips under me, chasing his own release and when he comes with a roar, we both collapse onto the ground, breathing heavy.

After a few minutes, I slide off him, dragging my leggings back onto my legs and wincing as I feel him seep from my body. My eyes land on Valentines' dead body, still and lifeless, his eyes staring straight ahead, the blooming puddle of blood growing bigger with every second whilst he just turns grey.

Lex grunts as he gets to his feet, leaning heavily to the left and pressing his hand to his shoulder. He'll live but I'm sure it hurts like fuck.

I prop myself beneath his arm to steady his walking and then head towards the door.

It bursts open before I can reach it and I find Ryker and King barging into the room, breathing fast and heavy.

"Where the fuck were you!?" Lex growls.

"On the other fucking side," Heart snaps back. "This building is practically a fucking maze!"

Ryker stares down at the dead enemy and instantly sags in relief. He's dead.

He's finally fucking dead.

"Leave him for the rats." Lex orders.

I didn't see any better way than that. He didn't deserve a 'clean up' or even an unmarked six foot hole. He was vermin food, nothing more and nothing less.

It was over with him.

We had won.

31.

Lex

After the doc finishes cleaning me up, I lay back onto the pillows, turning to face Wren who is curled on her side, freshly showered.

"Are you okay?" I ask.

She nods her head, "It feels surreal to be over."

I sigh. It wasn't over. Not yet. The syndicate are still at large, invisible and yet pressing in none the less. Heart is staying in one of the hotels in the city, waiting for me to come through with his payment and whilst he had told me he didn't want a war, I suspected his patience would only go so far.

"Rory was buried today," I tell her, cupping her face in my hand.

I would destroy the world for this woman, including my city, I'd level it all to have her right where she is now.

"Where?"

"In the Silver crypt," My finger strokes across her bottom lip.

"Thank you."

I nod. "I'll take you one day."

Images of the battle back at the hotel flash through my mind, Valentine with the blade against her neck, the manic and violent light shining in his eyes. Wren slicing through his throat like an avenging angel, watching as his blood coated her skin and never once grimacing or flinching. And then her riding me, urgent and chaotic. Her need filling me, pulling me up and the taste of her sweetness on my lips.

"Marry me." I say.

Her eyes widen, "Excuse me?"

"Don't pretend you didn't enjoy being called my wife, little bird," I grin, sliding my thumb between her lips, "be my wife. Be a fucking Silver officially."

She sucks at the pad of my thumb, tongue rolling around the tip and then she pulls away, "you want to marry me?"

"Yes, Wren."

She grins, "Shouldn't there be some grand gesture, you on your knees, a ring?"

"You want me on my knees for you, little bird?"

She cocks a brow playfully.

 With a grin to match hers, I slide from the bed, dropping to my knees, "I'm already there, baby," I admit. "I'll always be on my knees for you. I'd burn it all for you."

"I don't want you to burn it all," she breathes, leaning towards me.

"But I would."

"Yes," she whispers, "Yes, Lex, I'll marry you."

 The light of morning has started to bleed onto the horizon, turning the black sky grey and whilst a new day may be beginning there's too much shit hiding in the shadows.

I will be marrying this woman but only when this city is back under control. Only when I know she can rule at my side with no threats. I kiss her with the sun rising over our kingdom, and I vow to keep her as far from this as possible.

"Come now, Little bird," I coax, "stop asking so many questions."

She glares at me, lips pursed as I gesture for the door of the elevators. My eyes peruse her body, the smooth skin of her legs, the hem of her dress sitting just above the knee, long enough to cover the mark on her thigh, the skirt flared before becoming tighter on the torso, neckline high but not high enough to cover the sharp lines of her clavicles. Her mass of wild copper hair is pulled across one shoulder, untamable but it's her face that catches me off guard.

I expected some guilt over what she did last night, disgust or horror at herself for killing a man but her green eyes are clearer than they have ever been. She squares her shoulders and straightens her spine, tipping her chin to the ceiling, showing off that slice on her throat like it's a victory badge and not a wound that could have killed her.

She was going to be formidable.

"I don't like surprises," she grumbles reluctantly taking my outstretched hand. Her flat sandals hit the marble floor of the foyer and I press the call button for the elevator. I keep her hand in mine as we step inside and it takes her all the way down to the lobby.

"Where is everyone?" She asks as we walk across the spacious area, all windows looking out onto the bustling streets of Brookeshill.

"Who?"

"Well Ryker for one? Or any of your other men?"

"Why would they be here?" I smirk, turning just before the entrance doors and heading to a set of stairs that will take us to the underground parking lot.

"Well don't they come everywhere with you? Like bodyguards?"

I laugh at that, unable to stop myself I halt us on the stairs, grasping her and pinning her to the wall, ignoring the twinge of pain in my shoulder, "Do you think I need a bodyguard little bird? Who do I need protection from?"

Her cheeks flush and her lips part, a reaction to my proximity, "I just thought…"

"What kind of leader would I be if I couldn't take care of myself or my woman?"

"I don't need protection," she frowns.

"You are correct, but I'm going to give it to you anyway."

She kisses me gently and then pushes me off her body, tilting her head and raising her brows, "Where are we going?"

"You'll see."

I take her down to the Maserati, opening her door for her to step in, "Where were these manners when we met?"

I pinch my tongue between my teeth, "I'm not sure but I quite enjoyed having you restrained. Maybe we'll revisit that later, play a little."

Her eyes widen and then she shakes her head, averting her eyes.

I chuckle and close the door before rounding the hood and climbing into the front. The drive across the city is quiet, Wren watches the city roll by through the window until I'm pulling into a spot outside a huge building in downtown. She frowns but says nothing when I open her door and hold out a hand to help her from the car.

The building ahead of us is lavish and modern, and the door is opened for us, a man dressed in a pristine black suit waiting patiently for Wren to go ahead.

"Mr Silver," he greets me, "It is wonderful to see you again."

"It is not me you need to impress Mr Livingstone." I quirk a brow at the guy, noticing the light sheen of sweat dotting his forehead, the slight tremble in his hand as he reaches out to greet Wren.

"Miss Wren," he bows his head.

She takes his hand, "What's going on?"

Mr Livingstone frantically looks to me, eyes wide.

"Have you forgotten already Little bird?" I tilt her chin up, stepping between her and the old man, "We were engaged just last night."

"So?"

"So, an engagement usually comes with a ring."

"Oh," her plump mouth forms a little 'O' as she realizes what we are doing here.

"Pick anything," I tell her, "Or all of them, I don't mind."

She huffs out a laugh and shakes her head.

"This way, miss Wren," Mr Livingstone directs, "I think I have the perfect ring for you."

She frowns but follows after him as I watch on. They stop at a glass counter and he reaches underneath, unlocking the back to pull out a piece of jewelry I can't really see from this distance. Her fingers dart to her mouth to contain a gasp as her other hand whispers over the ring.

I gently step up behind her, looking over her shoulder.

The ring is beautiful, an oval cut ruby surrounded by glittering diamonds and a platinum band, the stones large but the ruby is truly a masterpiece. The deep red color reminding me of her wild hair.

"We'll take this one," I tell him.

"What?" Wren gasps.

"Of course sir," Mr Livingstone says quickly, "Is there anything else?"

I laugh, "Is there a set to go with this?"

"Yes sir, a necklace, earrings and bracelet."

"I'll take them all, also did you get that piece I asked you for?"

"Yes sir."

"Lex, you can't just buy that! Did you see the price tag!?"

"Do you like it, little bird?"

"Yes, of course, it's stunning but–"

"Then it is yours."

"But Lex," she starts but I cut her off with a kiss, "I'll buy you the whole damn store little bird if that is what you wish for."

"Lex," she breathes into my mouth.

"Sir?" I look over to the old man who holds out a set of jewelry on the counter, the ring holding centre place.

I pick it up, "We can resize if required," he tells me.

"Your hand, Wren."

She holds it out for me, and I slip the ring on to her finger, the band a perfect size for her dainty little fingers.

She stares at it, her hand resting in mine, the ring positioned and then looks to me, eyes glistening, "Don't go crying on me, little bird."

.

32

I stare at the ring on my finger, unable to withhold the emotion. How did this happen? How the fuck did we get here?

"Don't go crying on me, little bird," I look at Lex's face and I cry anyway. Lex swipes the drop from my cheek and places his thumb between his lips, tasting it. There is no regret there this time.

"Now you're always mine," he whispers and then turns me back to the set on the counter, the diamonds and rubies glittering where they sit in their velvet boxes. "Bag this up," Lex orders Mr Livingstone, "and bring me the last piece."

"What did you get?" I ask.

"You'll see," he grins.

When Mr Livingstone comes back out he places a rectangular box on the counter, opening it up to reveal a thin leather strap that has a wolf emblem and next to it, a feather.

He pulls the sleeve of his shirt up, showing his own cuffs with the same emblems.

"The wolf has always been a signet for the Silver family," he explains.

He lifts it from the box and positions it around my wrist, tying the leather strap. "All the Silver's wear them."

Whilst Lex pays for the jewelry I wait at the door, watching the city, still shocked at how we became this.

His captive turned fiancé. I was well and truly in love with the devil, the monster that haunts this city, and I was falling into his darkness. I thought I'd lose myself to it, to his abyss but I'm finding myself there instead. There are parts of me I didn't know existed, parts of me he has coaxed from the deepest parts of my soul. A protectiveness, a ruthless edge that appears whenever he is near. Not against him, but for him.

I thought murdering Valentine would haunt me. That my dreams would be bloody and violent but there's a sense of calm that has washed over me ever since I plunged that knife into his throat. A wash of serenity.

He's gone but I know Lex's battle is far from over.

I'll be standing at his side the entire time.

I'm here now, he wants me with him, on top, then I'll be right at the head of the war, standing next to the king.

My fingers play with the emblems on my new bracelet, pushing them both up and down the leather strap, "It suits you," Lex says, turning down the street towards the penthouse. His phone buzzes in the centre console but he ignores it, instead leaning over and grasping my hand, thumb stroking the newly placed ring on my finger.

After parking, we head up, a relaxed silence between us but I can almost feel the hum of anticipation vibrating between us. He's restrained but he twitches, fingers tapping against my skin.

I smile, knowing what's to come.

As soon as the door closes, I'm pinned to the wall, his mouth fused to mine.

"I'm trying to be better," he rasps, "but the moment that ring slid onto your finger I wanted you bent over and open for me right there on that counter."

"Don't be better," I urge, "never be better."

I feel him grin as his teeth nip at my skin, his phone buzzing again. Once again, he ignores it. He pushes up the hem of my skirt, hands skimming the intimate curve of my hip as his fingers squeeze my flesh. Heat floods me, warming my centre as he follows the line of my thong before slipping in the side and swiping against my clit.

"I love how wet you get for me, little bird, even when you didn't want to, you were so responsive for me."

I grind against his hand.

"Bend over," he rips himself away from me, "I want your ass in the air, little bird, let me see you."

"Where?"

"The couch," he jerks his head to the living area, "face the windows." I do as he orders, leaning over the back of the couch, placing my palms flat on the other side of the back rest. When he steps up behind me, he flips the skirt up and tugs my panties down my legs.

"You look so fucking sexy like this," he growls, tracing my spine with his finger, down to my ass and then through the cheeks before he slides that finger inside.

His phone buzzes again.

He drops to his knees suddenly and then buries his face between my thighs, tongue swiping at my clit with the full width of his tongue.

My legs threaten to give out at the sensation rocketing through me.

His phone starts ringing.

"Lex," I moan, trying to get him up.

"Shh," he whispers against my pussy.

He pushes one leg further out, sliding his hand down so it's cupping the back of my knee and then forces it up, opening me up further for him. "Don't move," he orders, taking that hand away and bringing it up, sliding two fingers inside me before putting his mouth to me again.

He sucks and he licks, pumping his fingers in and out of me curling them to tease at the sweet spot inside.

"Holy shit," I whimper, legs shaking, "Lex, I'm going to come."

This time when his phone rings I barely hear it over the roar of my blood in my ears but it's still there, that damn ringing phone.

"You taste so sweet, little bird," he rasps.

With the vibration of his deep baritone washing over me, mixed with the incessant flicking of his tongue, I come apart at the seams, shattering instantly. I cry out for him, but he doesn't stop until he's drawn every last second of my orgasm from my body.

Gently, he slides my dress back over my ass and helps me stand, my arousal still coating his mouth.

"That was just the start, baby," he grins wickedly.

His phone rings.

He rips the thing from his pocket, glaring at it, "What!?" he barks into it.

His jaw tightens with everything spoken down the line to him, his eyes pinning me where I'm barely held together, leaning against the couch.

"Fuck," he growls, "I'll be there in ten."

He hangs up and steps towards me, crouching in front of

me, "Unfortunately little bird, we are going to have to wait," he taps my ankle, sliding my foot into my underwear and helping them up my thighs. When he gets to my pussy he presses a gentle kiss there and then pulls the thong all the way up.

"What's going on?"

"It appears we have a package."

We walk down to the car whilst Lex explains the situation with the syndicate, from start to finish, "is Ainsley there?"

He shakes his head.

"Where is she?"

He shakes his head, "I don't know."

I have more questions than answers but don't voice them as we make our way to the compound, my mind whirling over all the information I've just been given. Lex's hands are tight on the steering wheel, his brows set low in a frown.

Is this what life is going to look like for us?

A constant battle.

Enemies around every corner.

My finger plays with the engagement ring on my finger, pushing it side to side.

The compound comes into view, the side of the house completely destroyed though it appears Lex has already had workers start on the rebuild.

There are several cars in the driveway, large black SUVs and a number of Lex's men hovering at the door waiting for orders.

The tension is wound tight but Lex even more so. The car crunches over the gravel and then he stops. Before he can climb out, I grab his hand.

His head whips around to me, a frown pulling down his brows. I lift his palm and press a kiss to his hand, "We'll destroy them all."

33

Ryker sits in the kitchen, nursing a scotch. He's staring down at a brown envelope in the middle of the table, sealed shut with no address on the front.

"When did it arrive?" I ask.

"This afternoon, a worker flagged me down when I came to check on the work."

"Hand delivered?"

"Mm," Ryker grunts, "We missed her."

I pick up the envelope and open it, sliding out a pile of photos.

Wren steps forward, looking over my shoulder as I begin to sift through them, my smile hardly contained at what I'm seeing.

People. *Important* people, all of them in precarious situations, I stop on one, the mayor of London, head buried between the thighs of a blonde haired woman when he has a wife and two children, a few politicians and high ranking CEO's. These people are from all over the world, huge cities, countries, there's even a fucking priest. I stop on one image, a guy in a suit, holding a gun to a woman, her son dead next to her.

"I thought they didn't get their hands dirty," I comment.

"I guess they will if they need to."

"Who is this?" I ask, tapping the photo.

Ryker looks over, "I believe that's Graham Edmonds, Edmonds Enterprises."

"Interesting," his reach is far, owning several well established and successful businesses across the world, a range of hotels and restaurants and is in real estate. I lift the envelope and tip it upside down, a flash drive thudding against the top of the table.

Without a word, I spin in the kitchen and head down to the office, hearing Ryker and Wren trailing behind. At the computer I load it up and slot the drive into the port, waiting for the contents to download. Wren stands at the other side of the office, looking around, taking in the paintings on the wall and the hundred-year-old whiskeys lining the shelves. She looks out of place and small, but I know this is exactly where she belongs.

Thousands of files drop, one by one, a list of sins to be used, extorted and bargained with. "She fucking got it all didn't she," Ryker comments, amusement lining his tone.

"She did." I agree and I knew exactly how to use it. Going through each file, I pull up tax evasion, drug and money trafficking, skin trade, everything and it's all tied to names. Names of the very people running cities, offices, senators, politicians. They're all corrupt. They're all dirty.

They were clever really, from the dates on these files, this has been going on for years and they've never been caught. There's never been an arrest. Most of their crimes are done using various different groups, some gangs, but I can see how they are taking over cities. Taking down the ruling bodies and inserting themselves in their place, taking over the drug routes, the money and gambling and inserting their own dirt, their own schemes.

Skin trade and trafficking is something us Silver's have never been interested in but the Syndicate, they were all for it. It was their main source of income and no doubt where Valentine got his inspiration.

A number of sex houses dotted around the world, girls used in various ways, images of them drugged, some dead, others frothing at the mouth all the while these guys in suits watch on with smirks on their faces.

I make a copy of all the information, saving it to a second flash drive and remove the drive.

This would take some time and I needed the Syndicate to come to me, I wasn't going to go looking for them.

With Valentine gone, they were probably making a new plan but this time, I'd be ready for them.

I store the flash drives in the safe in the penthouse and then go in search of Wren, finding her in the bathroom, drawing a bath. Her hand swirls through the water, mixing in bubbles, the stones in her ring glinting in the bright over head lights.

I press a button to dim them and then strip from the shirt I have on, wincing with the movements in my shoulder.

"All that shit I saw today," she comments as I brush her hair away from her face, "You're going to make them pay, aren't you? The trafficking, it's disgusting."

"It is, I agree, but organizations like the Syndicate are like a hydra, you cut off one head, three more rise to take its place. I plan on keeping them away from this city but I can't do much more than that."

"So it continues?" She grits her teeth.

"There's going to be plenty of shit in this life that you're going to see and not agree with, if you weren't here, it would still be happening, you would just be blind to it."

"I wonder if that would be better," she murmurs, switching the water off. When she turns to me her hands go to the large white bandage covering the bullet hole in

267

my shoulder.

She peels it away from my skin and finds a new one to replace it with, being careful not to disturb the stitches. When that is complete, she slips from her clothes, stepping over the rim of the tub to submerge herself into the water. A long exhale escapes her lips as she slips all the way down until the bubbles touch her chin and her lashes flutter against the apples of her cheeks.

I perch on the edge of the bath, watching her, patches of pinkened skin peeking through where the bubbles separate on the surface of the water. Perspiration dots across her forehead and a thin tendril of hair sticks to her clammy skin.

Reaching forward, I slide it off her face, watching as the water takes it.

"What's the plan?" She asks after a few minutes of silence.

"The plan?"

"For the Syndicate? How do you exactly plan to keep them away from the city?"

"Don't worry about that, little bird," I say to her, standing from the tub and heading for the door.

"Is this how it will always be?"

I stop in the threshold, looking over my shoulder, seeing her leaning out the bath, hands curled over the rim, watching me with narrowed eyes.

"What do you mean?"

"Keeping me at arms lengths? Married to you but not involved in your life? Do you expect a dutiful little wife?"

My lips kick up into a smile, "You are a lot of things, little bird, but a dutiful little wife is not going to be one of them."

She stands from the water, steam rising from her body and bubbles clinging to her skin, sliding over the smooth surface. Her eyes are narrowed on me.

"Then what will I be? If I am kept in the dark, what good am I to you?"

"You are not a pawn anymore."

"No, I want to be a player. I want to know what your plan is. I want to help."

"And I'd rather keep you here where I know you'll be safe."

"And what about you? You think I'm going to be happy day in day out, knowing something could happen to you?"

My chest twinges, I do understand but memories of her missing, away from me, the images and videos of her, beaten and tortured. It's the very reason I'd rather her stay away from this. Whilst the Syndicate wanted her dead because of Valentine, I cannot be sure they would not continue to make attempts now that he is gone.

I'm not suggesting her stay away forever, I knew a life like that would never satisfy a woman like Wren, but for now, I wanted her to be safe.

"I've lost you once," I sigh, "I cannot lose you again."

Her eyes soften as she climbs from the bath, wrapping her beautiful body in a white towel. She walks towards me, dripping water onto the floor before her arms wrap around my neck and she presses her lips to the centre of my throat, forcing my chin up.

"They would have to rip me from you," she whispers. "And I'd rather die than be away from you for even a moment."

34

Wren

I may not like what I am seeing, it may make my gut churn and my heart squeeze painfully inside my chest, reminding me constantly of my time spent with Valentine, but I can't stand back and watch it all from a sideline.

I need to be involved. I need to know I am doing something. Lex is right, I would be blind to it if it weren't for him and if what he says is true and that information is to be believed, the Syndicate is bigger than even Lex can take on. The idea that they would continue to get away with exploiting girls the way they were didn't sit easy but maybe, just maybe, this could be the start of their downfall.

They've been unchallenged for so long that us, the Silver's pushing them back may make others realize that they aren't so powerful after all.

I needed to be there, standing at his side, not for me, and not for Lex either, but for Rory and for all those girls down there in Valentine's keep.

I wanted to see them suffer for their hand in it.

Lex wasn't going to make it easy though and that pissed me off.

Have I not proven myself? Have I not shown what I am capable of?

I am not a weak little girl. I don't shy away from the blood or the violence, even when it makes my skin crawl, I watched a life be taken, I've taken a life. I can do this.

I *want* to do this.

I step from him, looking up into those pensive grey eyes, unable to read exactly what it is he is thinking.

When I think he may say something he simply steps from me and heads for the bed, unbuttoning his pants as he goes. I sigh, drying myself off and then dropping the towel in the hamper by the door, following him into the bedroom.

He lays beneath the comforter, hands behind his head, watching me, but I am watching the city. Even at this hour it is still alive, the streets below thumping with activity, cars and revelers and whilst the noise is muffled this high in the clouds I can feel that energy.

This is what it is to stand on top of a kingdom. To have the ground at your feet and the people before you bowing down to your every whim. Most of the citizens of this city don't even know that it is Lex that rules them, but should they step out of line, they will surely know who their king is.

I always knew there was darkness. Shadows. Demons.

I hadn't expected the level of corruption I'd witnessed but I am hardly surprised.

I step out onto the balcony, a smaller, separate version to the one in the living room, the cool wash of the night breeze cooling my heated skin. My hands wrap around the railings and I watch it all. I feel the burn of Lex's stare at my back but he makes no move to bring me back inside.

I stand for a little while longer, watching the world roll on by, realizing I'll never be the same again. I'll never have that innocence of believing the world was all sunshine and rainbows. I'll never be able to walk these streets without wondering about what kind of monster lurked in the shadows, beneath the ground and in all the dark corners.

I am forever changed and for it, I will be stronger.

I'll never be weak again.

I turn back to Lex, lounging on the bed, the muscles of his arms tense in the position he's in, veins snaking around his forearms and further up. Bronzed skin, glowing in the low lighting of the room and in even more stark contrast compared to the pristine white bedding beneath him.

I narrow my eyes.

I head towards the drawers on the other side of the room, reaching in to withdraw a dagger I'd found in here previously. Surely, he couldn't think I'd go long without exploring. The steel glints in the lighting, the sharp edge cutting into my skin as I run the pad of my finger across it.

"Wren," Lex growls.

I watch the blood bead and roll down the length of my finger before I cross the room and put a knee on the bed.

"You think I cannot handle what this life will bring," I say in a low voice, crawling up the bed, between his parted thighs where I then sit back on my heels, the blade held in front of me.

His eyes bounce from me to the knife, his brow cocking.

"And what do you think you're doing right now, little bird?"

I cock my head, my lips tilting up into a smile, "Reminding you of the woman you took all those weeks ago."

He smirks.

I crawl over him, straddling his thighs and then his hips, feeling the hard length of him through the sheets beneath my core.

"It really should disturb me that a woman holding a blade turns you on."

His hands come up to cup my sides before he suddenly yanks me forward, "What will you do?"

With my mouth whispering over his, I bring the blade up his body, purposely positioning the tip to face downward so it grazes over his bare abdomen as it goes. He hisses in a breath as the tip slices through his skin, and dropping my gaze down, I see a thin line of blood beading where I've cut into him. Barely anything, a scratch that'll close and heal in no time.

I stop and rest the tip of the blade against his throat, "I am stronger than I have ever been," I tell him, watching his pupils dilate, becoming so dark it almost drowns out the light, "More powerful."

"You are," his Adams apple bobs as he speaks, scratching the blade across his skin.

"And yet you wish to keep me in a cage?" I whisper, "Am I still your prisoner, Alexander?"

One side of his mouth tips up, "No."

"Then put me next to you," I demand, "Show them just how strong we are together."

I am no threat to him, the blade I hold to his throat is merely a prop, nothing but a thing that'll never be used against him. I mean I don't mind seeing him bleed a little.

"Formidable," he whispers before he strikes.

I am flipped, the knife knocked from my hand and

positioned in his and then pressed to my throat, "Well doesn't this bring back memories, little bird."

Instantly, warmth pools between my thighs. Don't ask me why but being dominated and subdued by him makes my stomach knot and my pussy clench like no other.

He grinds the length of him against me, the blade pressing just a little harder against my windpipe, "And what now, Wren? Are you still strong?"

"No," I breathe.

"No?"

When I shake my head the edge of the blade slices into my skin and I feel it come apart, blood welling and rolling over the surface, pooling in the little dip between my clavicles. Alexander snatches the blade away, "What the fuck!?" He growls.

"I am not strong here, Lex," I admit, "But neither are you."

His eyes snap from the blood on my throat to my eyes, widening, sensing the truth.

He had always been weak for me and would always be weak for me, but it would also be his strength and him, mine.

He had to understand how good we could be together if he truly let me stand at his side.

A duo to take down an army if only to protect our other

halves.

His mouth slams down on mine violently teeth nipping at my lips, tongues dueling.

"Okay," he rasps, "okay!"

His hips grind against me eliciting a low, guttural moan to rip from my throat.

"I love how responsive you are to me," he whispers against the shell of my ear before dipping his head to lick up the trail of blood on my throat. It stains his lips as he brings his head back to watch me through hooded eyes. "Always so ready, so wet."

I roll my hips, sliding over his length.

My eyes roll back as I go, the pleasure making my insides clench.

There's a clang of metal before his hands are dropping, tugging his boxers down his thighs.

"There'll never be enough time in this life to enjoy this," he growls before slamming forward, sliding inside me so deep I feel him in my stomach.

I cry out, my legs lifting and widening to allow him more access. He pulls out slowly, pressing his forehead against mine and thrusting his hips. One arm wraps behind my thigh, holding me in position and then he truly fucks me. Slamming in again and again, so hard my bones rattle and his mouth leaves hungry kisses against my throat, sucking and biting.

"Lex," I moan, lifting my hips a little to allow it in just that little bit further.

"Fuck," he rasps, "So good. So fucking good."

He fucks me hard, relentlessly, drawing an orgasm from my body so intense I'm sure I'll never recover and I know now, I know that he will accept this.

Despite whatever danger he believes I'll be in, he knows he cannot keep behind a shield.

Where he goes, I will always follow.

.

35

Lex

Wren stiffens next to me as we sit on the opposite side of the table, the restaurant around us busy, the talk loud and boisterous but the table we join is the complete opposite.

Kingston nurses a glass of wine as his eyes watch us take our seats before him. Isobel grins at Wren like a child might on Christmas morning and suddenly leans across the table, snatching Wren's left hand.

"Nice rock!" She beams, fingering the stones on her finger, eyes wide, "so pretty."

Wren carefully tugs back her hand, "thank you."

"You'll make a fierce queen," Isobel comments.

"It's taken you far too long to come to me with this information," Kingston muses, rubbing his bottom lip with his middle finger, the rings there catching in the light, "seeing as you've had it some time now."

"A few days," I agree, ignoring the fact that he already

knew I had it.

"And why is it only now I am seeing it?" He asks, flicking his eyes to Wren, "was my trade not valuable enough?"

My nostrils flare, "Don't push it, Heart, I don't care who you are, you're on my territory."

His laughter is light.

"Don't mind my brother," Isobel tuts, "he enjoys an argument far too much and does it often."

"It just seems that your brother is an asshole." Wren comments, her fingers curling into a fist atop the table as she glares at King.

"I am so very pleased I turned up when I did," King suddenly says, "A fire like yours should not be snuffed out quite as soon as Valentine had intended."

"Enough," I snap, "I have your information."

"I know you do," he leans back, waving over a waiter, "But let's eat first, I'm fucking starving."

I didn't have time for this shit.

I wasn't particularly fond of the Heart's. Kingston was infuriating but powerful, a ruler with an iron fist. With no information on the man, it made him unpredictable. He overthrew a notorious ruler for the throne, opened new trades and businesses in Europe and has never been challenged. Most don't like him, but they leave him be mainly because he'd flatten an army in a second and never blink an eye.

Isobel was chaotic. A charming and kind exterior that hides something a lot more insidious underneath. There's a darkness in her eyes that screams violence but again, like Kingston, no one knows much about her.

Even if I didn't like them, they were fearsome and respectable and I had to accept that this trade was worth it. He could have used Wren as a bargaining chip, blackmailed me into handing over the information, instead he did something not many men would have done in this line of work.

After ordering food, King forces the conversation onto lighter topics, steering away from anything Syndicate related. Wren has relaxed a little next to me, talking to Isobel about the tattoos that adorn her skin.

It's only after we have eaten and the restaurant has emptied a little more that he holds out his hand.

I pull the flash drive from my pocket and hover it above his open palm.

"What plans do you have with the information?" I ask.

"It does not concern you," King replies, "But I will not use it until your business with the organization is done."

"You're going back to the UK?"

"Tonight," King confirms, "There are matters to be addressed and I've been gone too long."

I drop the flash drive into his hand, "That has everything Ainsley uncovered, including scanned electronic copies of the images she got."

"Thank you," King dips his chin in a nod and stands, Isobel following. He steps away but stops at my shoulder, his hand suddenly falling there, "For the record, I meant what I said, I respect you and your family however," he pauses, bending, "I respect your woman a hell of a lot more for what she has endured. Take care of her."

And then they're gone.

"They freak me out," Wren comments, picking up her wine glass to take the last sip of red liquid in the bottom. Ryker drops himself into the vacant seats opposite us.

"I've ordered men to follow them to the airport, make sure they actually leave."

I nod my agreement, "Good, I want them gone before whatever shit goes down with the Syndicate."

"Do you trust them?" Wren suddenly asks.

"The Heart's?"

"Mm," she nods.

"Isobel is a bit of funny one," Ryker comments.

"They've kept their word," I say, "There's no reason for them to stay. I trust they'll leave, whether they come back…that's a different matter."

It's late, Wren and the city sleep but energy flows through my system making it impossible for me to rest. Too many variables and not enough intel keeps me on edge. With no idea where the Syndicate are or how many players they have keeps me awake. I trust my plan will be enough, an organization like that, with as many people as they have won't take a threat like this lightly.

The only problem, I didn't know how to find them and the waiting game was killing me. They would come, of course they would but *when?*

My fist flies into the leather bag, forcing it to swing violently against the impact and then I hit it again, trying to burn some of the excess energy.

"Lex," Wren's voice forces me to pause.

I grip the bag, stopping its swing and look at her from over my shoulder. My eyebrows rise at her attire, a pair of tight black leggings and a sports bra, her copper hair pulled into a ponytail that swings like a pendulum as she walks towards me.

"Trouble sleeping?"

"Something like that," I comment, eyes roaming down her frame, taking in the curves and mischievous grin pulling at her mouth. She is so much healthier now, her weight back to normal, the injuries healed or almost there.

"Spar with me," she says, taking a position on the mat, "burn some of that energy."

"I don't want to hurt you, little bird."

She laughs, "you won't hurt me."

She drops into a fighting position and raises a brow in challenge, "are you scared?"

"Oh, little bird," I laugh, joining her on the mat, "do you like a challenge?"

"Always," she grins and lunges for me, jumping so her legs wrap around my waist and then she throws herself back, bringing me with her. I suddenly fall forward with the momentum, hitting the mat on my knees but her body doesn't join me. She somehow manages to remove herself, leaping away and landing in a crouch in front of me, a smirk on her mouth.

I get back to my feet and crack my neck before I charge her, grabbing her around the waist to slam her down onto the mat, my hand cradling the back of her head to save it from the thump.

She doesn't lay there and take it, thrusting her hips up hard enough to wind me and then she flips me, straddling my hips with her hands around my throat.

"Too soft," she mocks on a whisper, "I'll win every time."

"Little bird," I rasp, my throat working under her palms.

"Yes, *my* twisted king?" She licks my bottom lip, "I'll accept a surrender if that is what you wish."

"Never," I growl, my fingers wrapping around her wrists.

And so we spar. We spar until we're too tired to go

anymore, too exhausted to think of anything more than just sleep.

And I forget everything until the morning sun wakes me and the trouble truly begins.

36

Lex

"They left," Ryker confirms standing on my left.

I nod, not saying a thing as I watch the man in the suit approach, followed by another who is far more threatening than the suit who stops a mere few feet in front of me. It isn't a coincidence that they sent word the moment Heart and his entourage were airborne.

Wren holds herself by my side, chin tilted defiantly.

"Wren Valentine," the man greets, looking her up and down, starting from her feet, all the way to the top of her head, "A surprise to see you so well."

My anger begins to simmer, just beneath the surface, not an explosion but I doubt it'll take long.

"You'd be surprised at what I am capable of," she snaps back, "Do not believe me weak just because I am a woman."

He licks his teeth, dismissing her before his eyes land on me, "You are proving quite the complication, Silver."

"Isn't that a shame," I lie.

He cocks a brow and grins, "I am here to talk of surrender, no more bloodshed."

Ryker bursts out laughing besides me and then sobers, "Oh, you're serious," he looks to me, "He's serious."

"You have the advantage of knowing my name," I say, "what is yours?"

"Eric Ward," he replies.

"Eric," I repeat, "What's your business?"

"A truce," he grins, "If you will."

My eyes flick to his man behind him, a mercenary, hired blade to make sure things here don't go sour. I didn't believe he was the only one available to him, I had no doubt there would be many, including a few snipers but as long as my plan worked, they'd all be leaving with no blood spilled tonight.

The compound is drafty, a late summer breeze drifting in through the gaping hole in the structure. "Valentine's body has been recovered," Eric tells me, spinning on his heel to start inspecting the space, running his finger over a shelf as if to inspect it for dust, "Quite the violent death."

"He deserved it." Wren says, her voice even and steady.

"Maybe so." Eric agrees.

"Speak your terms," I order.

"Surrender and no one else has to be harmed," he turns to me, "We can work out a deal where you continue to sit on a throne but ultimately, this city belongs to us."

"So, you can traffic more girls?" Wren steps forward, seething, "You are disgusting."

"You'll learn," Eric hisses, "You don't belong in these ranks, woman, you are nothing more than a wet cunt and easy lay."

"Enough!" I roar, "And if I do not accept?"

"Then you, your bitch and everyone involved will be seen to an early grave."

The way he says it, so calmly, as if a destruction of an empire is merely an everyday occurrence.

I was starting to understand though. They knew Ainsley had the information, but they had no clue that she had managed to deliver it to me already.

I had the advantage.

"Compelling words," I mock, "But I do not accept."

"Then you are a fool," Eric spits.

"Am I?" I ask.

Eric narrows his eyes, cocking his head.

"You see, I think I have something worth more than this city is to you."

Eric pales, "Is that so, Mr Silver?"

I hold a hand out and a simple brown envelope is placed there. Before I can even bring it to me a gun is drawn and aimed at my head.

"I wouldn't do that," I warn.

As if my words are a signal, the gun is aimed at Wren. She doesn't even flinch, if anything she stands taller and puffs out her chest, a cruel smile curling her lips.

It's the completely wrong time to get turned on but my dick twinges anyway.

Fuck, she's feisty.

"That'll end in much the same way." I tell him. "Should we see what we have here?"

The gun is not withdrawn but no shots are fired so I proceed. My heart pounds inside my chest. I don't care for my safety but Wren's. The barrel pointed at her makes me sweat though I keep it collected, cooling my expression as if the threat on her life is nothing more than an inconvenience.

I turn and head to the nearest surface, opening the

envelope and spilling the contents onto the side, revealing a number of compromising images.

"This is you, is it not?" I ask, fanning the photographs so each one can be seen.

Eric looks down at them, "This is nothing." He snaps.

I laugh, "No, but this," I pull my flash drive from my pocket, "this is enough."

"And what?" Eric laughs, "You'll go to the police?"

With everything backed up to my server I place the drive on the counter next to the images, keeping my hand over it, "No, but I will release it. I won't have to go to the police, I won't have to do anything at all. You've pissed off a lot of people over the years, before the police can even get to you or any of your associates you'll be ripped apart by the people and the families you've destroyed. They don't know who you are, they've never been able to figure it out, but this information will give them everything they could ever need."

With my hand still covering the drive I feel the cold metal of the gun press into my temple, "There is nothing stopping me." Eric warns.

I can't see Wren but I can feel her panic. I sense it down to my bones, feel her presence drawing closer.

"Do it. See what happens when I die." I laugh, "You're done, Eric. This city is gone."

"I don't think so. Shoot him!"
"No!" Wren screams.

"I die, it's released anyway." I rush.

I hear the safety catch, the movement of his clothes as he prepares to fire. The seconds that stretch between feel like hours but then Eric yells, "Wait!"

A long minute of silence stretches between us.

"What do you mean?"

"I mean," I turn into the gun, staring at Eric, "you shoot me, you shoot Wren, you hurt any one of us, then the world sees this. I have a clause in place, you see. I die, you do too."

"You're bluffing."

I wasn't, "Try me."

"So that's it?" Eric asks.

"You leave, I keep it safe, you stay away from *my* city, your information and your identities remain hidden from the public."

"How can you be trusted?"

"I can't," I admit, "But are you willing to take the risk?"

"How many people have it?" He asks.

"Enough."

"They wont like this."

"That's a shame," I say.

Eric waves a hand, disarming his guy but I don't relax, not yet.

"Ainsley," I continue, "She comes home."

"I can't do that," he says, "she's far too valuable."

"Then we don't have a deal."

"I can't promise you a single thing, Silver but I know your *Ainsley* is an asset."

"Then what can you promise."

"Your city." He growls, "We leave, in return you keep the information you have concealed."

"And Ainsley?"

"She belongs to the Syndicate now."

"No!" Ryker growls.

I had to think bigger than this. Ainsley was smart. Lethal. She could handle this.

"Fine."

"Fine!?" Ryker hisses.

I ignore him though I know he'll be pissed but this is

what needed to be done to take the enemy off our turf. I'll figure out another way to get Ainsley out of this mess.

"Do we have ourselves a deal?" I ask.

Eric pauses but then huffs, "Yes."

I don't dare relax, not until I watch the man exit my grounds and then have men follow him until he passes the city limits. I don't relax until I know he's far away from Wren and far away from me.

This city remains in the Silver hands and I'll be dead long before I see it anywhere else.

37

Wren

It doesn't feel like a win, it simply feels like we're pushing the inevitable.

My guilt ways heavily on my shoulders, guilt for Ainsley having to stay on the run and guilt for all those girls trapped inside the Syndicate.

The city may be safe for now, but I'll continue to push on Lex to do more.

Ryker sits on the couch, elbows on his knees staring out the windows whilst a scotch dangles between his fingers and Lex stands in the kitchen, pensive, brooding, thinking about everything that happened back at the compound.

I pass Gruff, touching his shoulder. He offers me a small smile but continues to stare out the window, no doubt thinking about Ainsley. I had to wonder what was going on there. Was it something more than just loyalty? When I reach Lex, I smooth a hand down his spine, feeling his muscles relax as my touch soothes him.

"Little bird," he whispers, dragging me forward until I'm in front of him and caged in his arms, his mouth resting in my hair.

"I think we should reach out to Kingston," I say after a few minutes of silence, "offer our help in taking them down."

"We aren't vigilantes," Lex mumbles.

"No, but I'm not comfortable leaving it as it is knowing what I know."

When Lex says nothing, I push from his chest and stare up into those steel eyes of his, "I'll do it myself. I don't need your approval."

His mouth tips up, "no, you don't."

"Okay, good." I nod once, "Then you won't mind that I've already contacted Isobel."

His chuckle rumbles through my chest, the vibration of it sending a swarm of butterflies to flutter in my stomach, "Why am I not surprised?"

I wasn't bluffing. I reached out to Isobel a few hours ago. After Eric left, taking his hired gun with him, I found their number and called her. She wouldn't go into details, she wouldn't tell me exactly what it is they were planning but she accepted my offer of aid should she ever need it.

Kingston still terrified me but I trusted he would do what was right in this situation.

Lex's hands skim down my sides as he leans down and kisses me gently, "Go on to bed," he tells me, "I'll be through in a moment."

I look to Ryker and then nod, leaving them to it as I head through to the bedroom and strip.

Rory would have wanted me to try everything I could to stop this organization. I didn't believe taking them down would put a complete stop to the exploitation of these women but I knew they were a big player and it would help.

Sliding under the sheets I turn to stare out at the twinkling lights of the city, the docks further beyond and let myself breathe for a minute.

How everything has changed.

How my life is a far cry from what it was only months ago.

I know I've made the right decision.

38.

Lex

"You threw her to the wolves," Ryker accuses, throwing back his scotch.

"Ainsley will be fine," I tell him, "But I have not thrown her to the wolves."

"What do you call it?" He snaps.

"What would you have me do?" I growl.

He sighs and places his face in his hands, shaking his head, and then he abruptly gets up, heading for the door without a word. It'll take him a few days but he'll understand I did what was necessary for this city.

When he's gone and the silence settles around me I finally stand and head for the bedroom, finding Wren tucked under the sheets in our bed.

Her wild hair spreads across the pillow, the color a stark

contrast against the white of the pillow.

It was over for now.

Valentine was gone, Wren was safe and the Syndicate have backed off.

I wasn't stupid enough to believe it was done, that they wouldn't try again but for now, I could actually sit back a little.

Stripping, I climb in behind Wren, pulling her closer to me. Her naked skin brushes against mine, warm and welcoming and when my hand runs down the length of her, she shivers under my touch, turning to face me.

I capture her mouth, kissing her roughly and pressing her back into the mattress, touching and tasting her skin.

Her fingernails scrape down my back, biting into my skin and I growl into her mouth, my need for her burning with each second that passes. I settle between her thighs, my cock pressing into her warm and sensitive flesh. Her back bows off the bed, her breasts pushed out and I capture a nipple between my teeth, nibbling at it as my other hand slides down her stomach before sliding through her folds and finding her clit. Her arousal smears across my fingers, making it oh so easy to tease her and have her panting under my weight. I slide a finger inside, capturing the gasp that leaves her lips with my own and unable to wait any longer, I position my cock at her entrance and slam forward, burying myself all the way to the hilt.

Her cries echo through the darkened bedroom, mixed

with the quickening tempo of skin hitting skin as I fuck her.

She was mine. She would always be fucking mine.

A queen.

The light in the darkness of my life.

"Lex!" She screams, widening her thighs but I grab one leg and force it back, lifting it so her ankle rests on my shoulder.

"Who do you belong to?" I grin against her mouth.

She laughs but it cuts off as I shift my hips, pushing in at a slightly different angle, rubbing up against that sweet spot inside her.

"Who?" I press.

"You!" She breathes.

"Do you want to come?"

"Yes!" Her nails claw at my skin, "Yes, *please.*"

I suddenly pull out of her body but before she can protest, I grip her hips and spin her, tugging her up so she's on her knees. My hand resting on the base of her spine, I reenter, the feel of her warm pussy enveloping me making my balls draw up and pleasure to shoot down my spine.

"Fuck," I rasp, sliding in deep and reaching around to

pinch her clit between my fingers. She bucks back, crying out but then begins to move herself, sliding herself up and down my shaft searching for that high.

I watch, my fingers working over her flesh as she becomes tighter and tighter until she finally snaps. Her cry of ecstasy echoes through the penthouse and when she finally calms, her body drops but I don't stop. I fuck her hard, pushing her body into the mattress with each deep thrust until my release stills my hips and I spill inside her.

With her head turned, she looks at me over her shoulder, breathing hard.

Slowly, I brush a piece of hair from her face, letting my fingers linger on her cheek before I lean in and kiss it, whispering into her ear, "Are you ready to rule, little bird?"

"With you," she sucks my finger into her mouth, "always."

Epilogue

6 months later.

The clip of my heels on the marble floor sets a steady beat as I descend the stairs and head towards the ballroom. A band has been set up in the corner, playing upbeat music but no one dances. Waiters buzz between bodies, offering glasses of champagne and tumblers of whiskey to the guests.

I spot Lex standing close to the bar speaking with the chief of police whilst Ryker leans against the wooden bar.

I start heading for him, the sight of him in his tux doing all sorts of weird things to my body. My dress, silver in color and tight at the top flows into a flattering A-line skirt that reaches my knees and my hair has been coiled away from my face, hanging down my back.

"Mrs Silver," A man stops my advance on Lex and I turn, narrowing my eyes at the gentleman.

"Yes?" I didn't recognize him but there were many faces I didn't recognize here tonight.

His eyes do a scan of my body, lingering a little on my stomach before he meets my face again, "I wanted to reach out," he says "I'm Detective Scott."

I cock a brow, "Okay?"

"I've been working on the missing girl case," he continues, "I understand you've had a lot of involvement."

I see Lex over his shoulder, eyes narrowed on the detective's back and it doesn't take him a minute to put his drink down and close down whatever conversation he's having with the chief to start making his way over.

"I haven't been all that involved," I say to the detective, "Merely provided some finance to help with the case."

"It has helped," he nods, "but I do not understand."

"What is it you're not understanding?"

"The men," he rubs his mouth, "we had leads and well now, they appear to be missing."

"Oh, that's a shame, what do you think happened?"

I knew exactly what had happened. It wasn't enough to simply have these *men* caught, they'll do time, not enough time and then walk away. That wasn't how I wanted this to work and Lex agreed. The police being involved was a complicated matter but a necessary one.

"I think you know," He grumbles, "your husband is not a good man is he, Mrs Silver? But you, you *were* good."

"I think you may be mistaken detective."

"Detective," Lex's hands comes down hard on his shoulder, fingers curling, "It's a little late to try and scare her off me, we're already married."

"Good evening, Mr Silver," the Detective snatches away from him, "I wasn't scaring her, just curious."

"Have you not got a case to crack?" Lex mocks, "now if you excuse us, my wife needs a drink."

Alexander takes my hand, tugging me gently away from the detective and towards the bar where Ryker waits. I do a quick scan of Lex's body, spotting the splattering of blood just beneath the lapel of his jacket. I huff, stop him and readjust the material, covering the evidence of his activities before the event started a few hours ago.

"You couldn't find a minute to change," I scold, pulling and smoothing the material down as I shake my head.

"I was late," he shrugs, "and we all know how my wife hates waiting."

"Why were you late?"

"There were complications," he simply says, "it got

messy."

"I can see that."

"It is dealt with now," he tells me, "what did the detective want?"

I grin, "Nothing at all really, inquiring about the missing leads."

After we tipped the police off to the missing girls and exposed an entire underground ring of skin trafficking in the deepest, darkest parts of the city we've been following and funding the investigation. The Syndicate had their hands in it but are still not directly linked but the biggest blow came when Lex discovered one of his most trusted men having his hands in the scheme. He knew he had a mole but he hadn't expected this one. Dawson and his family had been here for as long as Lex and his family had but Dawson wanted more.

"Trying to warn me that the man I am married to is not a good man."

"He is not," Lex agrees, leaning down to kiss me tenderly, "But he is utterly devoted."

When he pulls away, he does a scan of my body, hands coming forward to rest on the growing bump on my abdomen. He smooths and tightens the material of my dress, revealing the swollen area before he rests his hand over my naval, rubbing his thumb in circles.

"Have I ever told you how beautiful you are pregnant?"

"Only a few hundred," I laugh, leaning into his hand.

"I'll be sure to keep you this way for a few years."

A laugh bursts from me, "I think not, this one is enough."

"Oh no, little bird," he teases, "I'm thinking at least three."

I shake my head, his hand gently caressing my bump before he guides me and sits me in a stool at the bar.

"You realize there is an audience," I breathe as his mouth descends onto mine, his tongue slipping between my lips.

"Let them watch," he rasps, "It can't help just reminding them all that you belong to me."

"Like they could forget."

"So much sass, Mrs Silver," he tuts, "do you enjoy spoiling all my fun?"

I push him away though his hand still lingers on my stomach. It's been like that since he found out I was pregnant the day after our wedding.

He promised me I'd always be his first. His only. His queen and he's kept his promise. Just like I promised to always fight him but love him later, to be his light even on the darkest of nights.

But there was one thing I was certain of. No matter how

hard or dark our life got, I'd always stand by his side.

The End

Of course, it's not over… Wren & Lex may have their happy ending but we are only just getting started.

Keep an eye out, Kingston's book is next!

COMING
2022

WICKED
HEART

A WRECK & RUIN NOVEL
RIA WILDE

Acknowledgements

Firstly, I just want to thank every single one of my readers. When I first started this duet I never expected it to take off like it did and that's all thanks to you. Thank you for taking a chance on my books and thank you for all your kind words and encouragement.

A huge thank you to all the book bloggers, bookstagrammers and booktokkers who signed up to help promote this book! All of you have helped me so much over the last few months that I don't think any amount of thanks will be enough!

To Emma - without you and your constant nagging (in the most loving way of course) I would not have been able to complete this book earlier. Thank you for listening to me rant and kicking me up the ass when I doubt myself. But mostly, thank you for just being you and always being there. Anna - You're amazing! Thank you for loving Little Bird so much you slipped right into my DM's! Thank you for being one of my betas on this book, I needed all your words of encouragements!

To my husband, who believed in me right from the beginning. You've listened (kind of) whilst I've babbled about plots and characters. You've helped and pushed me when I needed it the most. I love you

ABOUT THE AUTHOR

Bringing you stories that are dirty, dangerous &
deliciously sinful.
Ria Wilde is an indie author who writes dark & sinful
romance. A lover of all things gritty & dark, the anti-
heroes we all hate to love and of course, the
possessive alpha men. When she isn't writing, you'll
likely find her with her nose in a book or doing her
second love, graphic design!

Printed in Great Britain
by Amazon